'Easy does it, Lee.' Farrell grabbed his kit bag and towel and headed for the showers. 'You're revealing too much of your hand. If this were a card game – '

Lee Wolf's fingers gripped Farrell's arm. Farrell turned and looked into a calm and confident gaze. 'This isn't a game, James. I'll say it again. I have nothing to hide. I'm not *playing*. I'm working. The facts stand: if we are not earning money, we are dying. And we are dying. And I'll tell you something else. Six members of the board agree with me. This phase of Shane Longman is over. Ansen and Company have to go!'

A moment's fragile silence followed, both men zinging. 'You won't unseat me, Lee. I'll be here till I'm dead.'

'That suits me fine, James.' He smiled. 'So what about the postponement of a meeting?'

'Sure, if you like. I'll take my chances on Ansen's team. My guess, they'll turn in some figures that will take the steam out of your paper.'

'You have great faith.'

'Yes,' James Farrell said. 'I do.'

MICHAEL FEENEY CALLAN

Capital City

Based on the series created by
ANDREW MACLEAR

Thames Mandarin

For Corey Wilson Callan

A Thames Mandarin Paperback

CAPITAL CITY

First published in Great Britain 1989
by Mandarin Paperbacks
Michelin House, 81 Fulham Road, London SW3 6RB
in association with
Thames Television International Ltd
149 Tottenham Court Road, London W1P 9LL
Copyright © 1989 Euston Films Ltd & Michael Feeney Callan

ISBN 0 7493 0115 5

A CIP catalogue record for this book
is available from the British Library.

Phototypeset by Input Typesetting Ltd, London
Printed and bound in Great Britain
by Cox & Wyman Ltd, Reading

CONTENTS

ONE

Mayday

Dawn is a bastard. Especially when the woman you are sleeping with – or rather, not sleeping with – is the wrong woman and it should be moistly warm but it's dry and airless and cold as interplanetary space. Declan McConnochie looked across at the bedside mirror, aimed strategically in some long forgotten moment of voyeuristic ambition, and saw himself. He saw a handsome, jaded face and eyes without emotion. When he thought the word 'emotion' dominoes fell and he thought about Michelle so he crashed gears and edged himself up in the bed, disturbing the redhead called Collie. All night long he had wanted to rouse her to tell her what a damn silly name Collie was, but that energy would be redundant. She came, was fed; she played, would leave. There would be no analyses, no promises, no recriminations. She was a bigger gunslinger than even he. Whoever said sex and sentiment were joined at the hip? Thank God for Emmeline Pankhurst and Tom Crabtree. It was just another night.

But it wasn't just another night. It was a night of numbness on the heels of a day full of aggravated tensions, when the bitter fruits of a mistake he'd made were coming down in an avalanche, threatening to pulverize him. He had hidden away from the city for a day and crowned that day with the insouciant Collie, but now the body clock of his beloved routine had him, he could hide no more. He turned on the hot shower and the boiler barked out last night's boiling water.

Collie stirred in a heap of Laura Ashley, a Christmas gift from Michelle, and opened her orange lashes. 'Ah,' she said.

'Coffee? Tea? Flakes? Grapefruit? Honey – ?' He liked the naked dawn air round his breakfast body when he had slept, hated it on nights like these.

'Goochie Conn'chie,' she said. 'You haven't slept enough. Come back to bed.'

'What? And miss this?' He whipped back the drapes and the peasoup dawn came in. He resented her abbreviation of his name and regretted her memory of it. He hardly knew her, had met her in the Spanish Steps, one of his places. He had wanted to bed her because he had never bedded a redhead nor an Irishwoman. She was both. She was as dramatically disappointing as he expected. He would not want her to call him. She would try Shane Longman but he would tell reception, alert Hannah, build the ol' smokescreen. Susan and Hannah and the boys would nudge and grin and Michelle would send him that look, but never say a word.

He pulled her from the bed protesting. 'What were all the world's charms to mighty Paris, once he found that dawn in the arms of his Helen?'

'You are so romantic.' She held him, like a limpet.

'Come on,' he coached. 'Remember what Napoleon said: a man needs four hours, a woman needs five and a fool needs more.'

She cooed. 'We only had an hour.'

'I don't mean that!'

She ground into him and he hesitated. 'Feel you; you're all wound up. Yesterday was nice but last night was too fast. My head was all woozy. I wish we'd talked more. I could talk to you, I could.' She rubbed her forehead against his frown. 'You have a lot on your mind, right? You're tired and it's six o'clock – '

'So late already? I'd better shift it.' How do you stand naked in a ramshackle Islington flat and tell a woman you have a debt of seven hundred and fifty grand bearing down on you and that time has run out? Where do you begin to explain a dealer's lot?

The phone went and he wanted it to be Michelle. She knew his rattlebag Audi had been in the Hyde Park pound since Sunday because he'd left a message on her machine – for every reason and for no reason, like always. Maybe she had missed him yesterday? Maybe she was ringing with bated concern, offering a lift? But it was Wendy Foley, the head dealer at Shane Longman.

'Wendy?' Collie vaporized in his arms and his upper lip was suddenly sweating. Wendy was thirty-four, a trader at Chase Manhattan since she was twenty-two, a Taurean, a snip from Vogue, a bull. She always made his pulse move.

'We didn't see you at the bank yesterday.'

'I had sinusitis and had to see someone. Harley Street. Sometimes it gets so bad – '

'See us today.'

The line went out and Collie said something but all he could see was Jimmy Destry, the small bastard, with his East End chip and his novelty ties and his promise to take back the ten year notes and relieve the death sentence.

He went back into the shower and stood under the spray. His eyes were raw, his body wired. He couldn't sleep for maybe another twenty hours. As he washed there was a neutered calm about his body that enraged him.

'Declan?'

He came out, towelling down. She looked scared, a rabbit caught in the headlights. 'The hardest part of anything is the beginning.'

This was worse than dramatically disappointing. This was a surprise. 'I'm sorry,' he said slowly. 'I'm a bum. I like fast motors, the occasional bottle of the Widow, good satin underwear and faraway beaches. But most of all I like what I do – '

She looked around the apartment: at the collapsed antiques that he had promised himself to restore, at the unread towers of books, at the knots of clothing. 'This?'

'Don't be deceived. Inside my head are palaces. Ambitions. I don't belong here.'

He expected a sneer, the angry flash of incisors. But instead her face softened, became radiant. 'You're not a bum. You're a good-hearted kid playing adult games . . . and they're beginning to bore you.'

There was a question tucked in her smile but he swerved away from it. 'I shouldn't comment,' he said.

She reached for her clothes. 'Whoever she is,' Collie winked, 'she's a lucky lady.'

Nothing in the *Buddhacarita* prepared Wendy Foley for days that started like today. It was her custom to rise at five thirty, feel, feed and interview her Hampstead

houseplants, do up her special Ethiopian Mocha coffee,
light a candle and dip into Buddha – all before breakfast.
Asvaghosa's poetic text, which was her refuge and
inspiration, had ironically been introduced to her by
her husband Bruce, he who had long since departed in
a cloud of very un-Eastern hysteria. Each dawn she read
and meditated, and by six o'clock her cardiovascular
rhythm was Swiss, her thoughts honeyed: she was
ready for anything the City could throw at her. But
today was different, today defied Enlightenment.

At six fifteen she was brewing the coffee (twenty
minutes late: unforgivable), scalding the cat and cursing
like a navvy. A lot of the damage was self-inflicted.
She'd been sloppy lately, missing some beats that
Threadneedle pros can *never* miss, shutting down her
instincts. And the missed beats spelt trouble. Witness
Howard Allen, corporate headhunter, professional
Errol Flynn . . . and currently hammering on her front
door. Only six hours ago she had chastely kissed him
goodnight and run from his car to her house reflecting
on a relationship that, for her, was out of control.
Howard was lovely, a gingerbread friend, but not for
smoochy late suppers and early mornings. Where and
when did she overstep the safety zone? More importantly, why?

It was four and a half years since Bruce had come out
of the closet and confessed that his truest love was a
football player called Nick. After the disbelief and deri-
sion came the hurt and the long aching twilight of
acceptance. Seven years with Bruce, seven years of
laborious brickbuilding, striving for the money and the
options, the power and the freedom, the golden kids
and the house-on-the-hill. But with the growing acceptance came growing strength. At the day's end she had
a splendid house – or rather, her legal half of it – and

a lesson: trust no man. All men have two independent personas: head- and groin-based. What untrained woman can handle such schizoid duality? Lines were drawn. There were male friends, but no boyfriends. Handshakes, but no hugs. She liked the way it now was, but here was Howard upsetting everything, tilting a perfectly good platonic relationship into areas uncharted and unwanted.

She opened the kitchen window and called down to him furiously, angry more than anything that her train of urgent thought – business thought – had been broken. She'd slept late, her rhythms disturbed by the later-than-usual night with Howard, but had jolted awake with a five forty call from the office that had her buzzing. It was Hannah Burgess, Administrator of Settlements and Computer Systems at Shane Longman – the woman, legend had it, who never left the bank building. Hannah had been apologetic, embarrassed: 'Wendy, I'm sorry to get you so early and I know it's not my place to be calling you, but Mr Wolf wants you – '

'At five forty?'

'He was afraid you'd be having a clients' day. Your diary looked full – '

'So what's the flap?' But she knew the flap. Wolf had summoned her yesterday and she'd failed to show – not through wilful indifference, but because she was busy paddling. All last evening the guilt of her discourtesy had hung over her, but she wasn't about to show it to Hannah. 'Listen, Hannah, if I don't make an appointment there's a damn good reason. Lee Wolf knows that. All this tactical rank-pulling doesn't impress me. I'll be in the building at six forty-five. I'm always in the building at six forty-five, he knows that. He's an executive director, fine. He's the Corporate

Finance man. But that doesn't mean he runs the whole show.'

There was a positive gulp down the line. Hannah, peace-seeking Hannah, would be glowing pink. 'Wendy, I'm just trying to help – '

'Tell him there are such things as reasonable business hours.' She rang off and pulled away from blethering rage, but the chain reaction of intensified concerns kept her from the *Buddhacarita* and the tranquillity required for her daily meditation. At five fifty she did try to dispel her tension in a plant-watering bout, but then Ansen rang. His was a voice, a presence, that she loved and hated at once and her confusion always manifested itself in a stern combativeness.

'What is it?' she demanded. 'World War Three has broken out?'

'You had Lee Wolf?'

'I had Lee Wolf's gofer.'

'He stepped off a plane from Wall Street yesterday, full of the fury and wisdom of Kuhn Loeb, Lehman Brothers, you name it – '

'The second quarter figures?'

'Got it in one. He's appalled. Says our performance so far this quarter is, quote, "indefensible".' *Our* performance. Maybe that was the part of Leonard Ansen that Wendy most loved. The open-handed sharing. As Senior Director of Banking Activities he was a heavyweight executive many pegs above her. He was entitled to bring her to heel, spike his dialogue, elbow the blame. But he rarely if ever did. She had known him nine years, since his time at Chase Manhattan where his restructuring of the Capital Markets had set the world on fire. She was at Chase Manhattan in Eurobonds at the time, but their professional friendship had been close and immediate. After a management shake-up Ansen took Wendy away from Chase and found them both desks at Shane Longman. At the time he apologized for what he called 'the comedown'.

That had been a couple of years ago. Today Shane Longman had a capital base of more than five hundred million and romped with the best through Foreign Exchange, Loans and Deposits, Capital Markets, Corporate Finance, Mergers and Acquisitions, Venture Capital and Equities, much of its progress being directed by Ansen. Still a minor leaguer, the bank had the admiration of the big City institutions and the words 'vibrant', 'innovative' and 'daring' were often on the lips of peers and competitors – as often describing Leonard Ansen and his tacit personal plan as the bank itself.

'We're doing our best in a tough market,' Wendy said. 'Everyone's taking a beating. It's just the time.'

'Wendy, I know. And you know we're in the same camp. But we *need* to show black ink now.'

The desperation rang like a klaxon. 'That's a lot of emphasis, Leonard.'

'You know me, I know you. We have a way, OK? Some people would call us unorthodox. You have no accounting to me as head trader other than what you want to do, right? I give you room, I trust you.'

'What are you saying to me?'

'I'm saying that Lee Wolf has gone past being a bad joke. He's a good man, he has sway. And he's got Ralph Goldring.'

'Tell me something new.'

'All right I will. Cabals are forming. There are people who no longer like the way we do business. People who think our style puts the whole show at risk. I give you the room to take on mavericks – mavericks like Hudson Talbot, or Max Lubin, or that kid Jimmy Destry, or Declan McConnochie. They earn big, sure. Sometimes they bring us sterling scalps. The Onocco deal, the Teacher's Retirement Plan – all that. But the trouble is, they swing the other way too.'

'Hudson and Max are doing just fine.'

'But some of the others – Destry and McConnochie – maybe not so fine and you know it.'

'You want me to ditch them?' Her voice became crisper, open combat. 'Because if that's what you're saying – '

'Easy, girl. I know your loyalties. But life is not charity. Wolf and Goldring are banking on bad second quarter figures to set the seal on a paper they're preparing called "The New Trading Profile". Do I need to spell it all out?'

Wendy poured her coffee and drank it bitter-hot. 'Under the circumstances I think it's very generous of Lee Wolf to fire a shot across the bows.'

'So do I. Thing is, Wendy, I'm happy where I am. I intend to stay put. You're my lady and you have your boys. They've got a job to do and it's up to you to see they do it. Like, right now. We've got about a week.' The line went dead.

Any hope of organization and relaxation went to hell after that – and now here was Howard Allen with his intrusive, loud-mouthed friendship.

Wendy changed her robe, pulling on a less enticing towelling button-up, and let him in. The desired effect was not immediate. He hugged her, kissed her hair, told her effusively how Cole Porter perfect his evening had been. 'I had to hit the trail early,' he gushed, 'and I know you're an early riser, so I thought – why not call round?'

'I appreciate the thought – '

He frowned. 'But it doesn't make you happy?'

'I'm sorry, Howard, I just had Lee – '

'Lee? As in Big Bad Wolf?' He was on a roll, targeting the coffee and toast. 'He's misplaced, Wendy. He's a born asset stripper, not management material. When he left Citibank we all put our money on an assets move. But then the word was he wanted Shane Longman, driving seat, kit and caboodle. Now if only James Farrell would drop dead – '

She didn't want this intimacy. In an instant, in the calm familiarity of his glide around the kitchen, it offended her. She removed the coffee pot from his grip and he recoiled, blinking. 'It's nice that you're interested in what goes on, Howard – '

'It's my job.' His face was suddenly studious and severe.

'And it's my job to keep my business to myself. I think we should define boundaries.'

He gave a forced laugh. 'You mean you're not inviting me to move in?'

'I'm going to sell, Howard.'

The smile froze in his eyes. All that remained was a cold dummy-like grin. 'I have to admit I had hopes – '

'I'm going to split it with Bruce and stop pretending.'

'Pretending what?'

'That the past lives. I don't want a relationship, Howard. I don't want marriage. I don't want late night and early morning commitments that get in my way. I'm a career girl and all I want is Shane Longman.'

He looked at her with a flinty stare that made his face someone else's face, a mystery man. 'You're a rare beast, Wendy. I can't imagine letting you out of my sights.' He didn't lift the half-filled coffee cup. 'I suppose I should be elsewhere,' he said.

Hudson J. Talbot III's Mayday call from Wendy came

at six thirty, slap in the middle of the greatest crisis of his personal life. He took it in the half-built library, seated under the perfect row of newly-fashioned lancet windows that looked down on Highgate. When he rang off he found himself tilted forward in his chamois swivel, mouth agape, in mesmeric concentration on the gilt-framed photograph of Alex that hung on the opposite wall. The picture absorbed him as it always did – the icon, the focus of their whole life together. That was the first time he travelled with her, on a JAL promotions junket. Always, when that tableau came alive, he remembered first the pride.

The pride of the first night party at the Tokyo Hilton, or the bus ride from Osaka to Kyoto, where all the children chimed together to sing a song to her beauty. It wasn't simply the fact that she was a much-applauded international model and all men wanted her – it was more than that; even the children loved her, and sensed all the goodness and warmth that he saw. He remembered too the pride he had felt on introducing her to Dad and Mom, in silvery retirement in Singapore. It was a long time since Litchfield, Connecticut and the stud farm and the everyday urgency to impress Dad, to prove he was more than just the kid with the golden spoon; but he felt like a kid again when he went up to the house over the bay and said, 'Dad, this is Alex Lavell, this is the girl I'm going to marry.' Nothing had impressed Dad more – not the laurels of Harvard, nor the independent move to London, nor the glittering successes as a Capital Markets man on the floor of various important City banks. Dad adored Alex (who seemed to win *all* men over), and Mom found her 'special'. Pride and love became all tangled up, but he knew she loved him so he felt secure when they married and she quit her agency. They settled down to a London life where his career and the sterling-dollar were paramount.

They had had good years and now they had a good house, a wonder house, designed by them both and nearing completion. More than half a million had already been sunk in the property, the mortgage was hefty, but the hundred-grand-plus salary from Shane Longman made the going easy enough. These very walls, in their grandeur and harmony, were a monument to a unique and beautiful love. And if that wasn't luck enough, their first child, a boy called Jamie, had arrived punctually nine months after the wedding, and stolen everyone's heart. It was a masterwork of bliss, a charmed world, a dream life. Hudson J. Talbot had it made.

Hudson pulled himself back from Kyoto and studied the fax contract from the Paris agency on the desk before him. He read again the line: 'Ms Lavell agrees to support and supply all promotional duties as directed by the agency . . .' It was innocuous, but it was also a death sentence. He frowned and tried again to blank out his suspicions. There was a tap at the door and Alex entered. 'The phone?'

'It was nothing.' He smiled and crossed to hold her. 'How's my son?'

'Sleeping. We need to find that nanny. Since Betty left – '

'But I like you mothering him. It's nature. It's the way it should be.'

She looked crookedly at him and for the thousandth time he wished she'd fight. Alex never fought, never disputed, never frowned. Alex was a model girl, a model mother, a model wife.

'I don't think I can skip out today,' he said.

She winced and he thought for a fleeting moment

that she was in physical pain. 'That's all right,' she said. 'It's the banking business, isn't it?'

'But it's not all right,' he returned. 'Shane Longman takes up more and more of my life – '

'Will you stop worrying yourself! I'm perfectly able to keep myself occupied. So, we miss another day. We can pick up. Now stop fussing.' She saw the offered Paris contract and snatched it up with a gesture that cherished and hid it all at once. He saw, and his stomach lurched.

'I don't want you to do that,' he said. 'Paris can wait.'

'I know.' She said it airily, not looking at him, not caring.

She turned for the door but he sprang from the chair and intercepted her. He held her arms tightly and felt her stiffen under his gaze. 'Say something unkind,' he demanded. 'For Christ's sake say *something*, Alex. Tell me you want to take it. Tell me you miss the adulation and the excitement and now this offer has come up and it has changed your life – '

A sparkle like tears lit up her eyes. 'That is nonsense, Hudson. I love you. I do not and did not love modelling. Yes, it is nice to be asked again. But I don't want to do it. I never had the temperament for modelling . . .' Her eyes suddenly refocussed on him. 'I wonder, do you know that? I wonder, do you know how my mind works at all?'

'You miss it?'

'I miss you.' She cupped his face tenderly but he pulled her hand away.

'Tell me that I have no practical skills, that I'm a nuisance round the house, that I can't cook, that I irritate you in bed – '

'This is the most absolute nonsense, Hudson. What is troubling you? Eurobonds have crashed? Max has led you into a blind alley? Was that the phone call?' He didn't speak, just stared dumbly and suspiciously at her. She gave her reassuring, practised smile. 'Was that it? Wendy Foley, the usual crisis? Well don't let it get to you. You always work the miracle and twenty-four hours later you're talking bonuses.' She looked endlessly and deeply into his eyes and gave a sad little smile. 'That's what you exist for, Hudson, isn't it? Those crises, those bonuses?' She waited for a reaction but he was lost on another track, a million miles from her. He was jealously thinking of the offered contract, that absurdity. She shook her head, suddenly sure that she would never reach him. She pressed his hand. 'Now, come on, cheer up. I'll fix breakfast in the sun room. It's lovely. The geraniums are thriving. The window boxes look like Gstaad.'

When she left the room his blood was boiling so fiercely that he sat and put his head between his knees and did the snatch-breathing exercises he had learned at the gym. Then he got up and walked the long rectangle of the Persian carpet again and again till his pulse evened out. What had fractured so tragically in their relationship? Was it, simply, communication? Might it possibly be that the demands of Shane had muffled their chances and they had drifted too far apart. In some strange way, some indefinable way for Hudson, the baby made matters worse. Whatever spontaneity they had once shared was gone, the signs and signals were no longer direct. That she was dissatisfied, he was in no doubt. But the precise reasons for her dissatisfaction confused him. The easy culprit was the agency offer. But was that too easy and too obvious?

Still unshaven, Hudson caught his reflection in the lancet window and shook himself. He thought of Wendy Foley and the gravity of her call. Only very rarely did Wendy show her jitters and when she did an all-systems response was the *only* response. He liked Wendy, appreciated the fact that she had gone out on a limb to make a job for him when the one big disaster of his career – the Fordham shares collapse – put him out of Threadneedle Street. Wendy was the one who took him in as Capital Markets Originator, perhaps *the* key analyst on the dealing floor, and after Fordham's that was one helluva gesture of faith. No, 'liked' was too subdued and British a word; he loved Wendy for giving him back his career graph and the notes that made it possible for him to put Alex where she should be, in a princess property overlooking Highgate.

Hudson crushed aside his sense of crisis and ran upstairs to shave. As he crossed the hall on noiseless bare feet he stalled. A strange and frightening sound, a murmured agony, came from Jamie's nursery. He moved to the door and gently tipped it open. Alex was there, on bended knees, with the baby cuddled in her arms, rocking him back and forth, weeping her heart out. Her back was turned, but he was tempted to run to her, to grab her and blanket her pain. He was tempted, but in an instant, in the flexing of a single muscle, he knew it was not possible. Nothing he could say or do anymore could assuage her unease. She was out of reach to him, she was gone.

'Here's your train.'

The Glasgow departure was again announced over the tannoy and the Euston crowds eddied. But Mrs Ewell stood her ground.

'Listen, Mum, Jimmy Destry said he'd pick me up. If I don't go now he'll move without me – '

'You don't want to hurry around for that fellow. He's cheeky, Chas. I wasn't impressed.'

'He's fine. We've shared the house for six months and we only argued once.'

'That's because you always give in. It's like your father says, being here in London you're givin' in.'

Here we go again, Chas hummed; but before he could apply the mental brakes he was back on that old roller-coaster, back self-justifying and pleading all at once. 'Mother, I like it in London. I like the money – '

'How much?'

'I told you. I'm taking about forty-two this year. That's forty-two grand, plus bonuses – '

'And the taxman eats you alive.'

'The taxman eats everyone alive, Mother. And are you going to try to tell me Dad earns as much in Scotland?' He cast a wry sideways glance. 'Tell me if I'm wrong. What does Dad earn as a match factory engineer? Seventy, eighty?'

'No need to be cheeky, laddie. Everything in life isn't pounds, shillings and pennies.' She dropped her voice to a conspiratorial whisper. 'Mind you, your father's no idiot. What he has earned he's put into – ' She looked warily around, seeking eavesdroppers, 'Krugerrands.'

'I could give him some sounder options.'

'Chas, you're wasting your life. I know people who've done what you and that Jimmy Destry are doing. Robbie McDermott, his brother Angus. They joined the bank in Edinburgh and came home in their flashy Bentleys. Next thing you know they're under lock and key. In prison, I tell you – '

'Oh for God's sake, Mother. You're going to miss your train.'

The bluster died and suddenly her eyes were wet and sincere. She held his hand and its soft fragility shocked him. His mother, this tigress, and yet she was crying, and shaking. 'Sonny, I'm sorry. I'm sorry if I made the last three days miserable – '

'Don't be silly. I haven't seen you since Christmas. I miss you and Dad and the old place.'

'And we miss you. *He* misses you, Chas. That's my biggest worry – him comin' out on retirement next year and you not being there for him. You're the light of his life, you know that.'

'I know the way he is.'

'Will you do something for me, laddie? A special favour?'

'Mother, don't ask me anything I can't deliver.'

'Come home. Just for a wee while. He has a week or two due, a bit of a holiday. Come back to your roots and be with him.'

'When?'

'Now. This weekend. That's all I ask. Just for a fortnight.'

'If I go back, London is lost. You know Dad. It took me three years to get the zest to get here. I've been here three years. And in that time I've built half a nest. At Shane Longman I got my opportunity – '

'An opportunity for what? For ulcers.' She shook him. 'Just this fortnight, son. For me.'

The guard's final whistle sounded and the last travellers dashed aboard. Chas lurched his mother to the open door and pushed her inside. She kissed him and squeezed his hand and without saying yes he said yes in a blink and a wave, and then she was gone.

Chas turned back along the platform with leaden feet. Already he was rehearsing the struggle with Dad, all the macho awful games they played. He glanced at his watch and knew it was too late for Jimmy Destry. Jimmy wasn't the waiting kind. Already he'd be burning

rubber down Threadneedle Street, seeking the unfind-
able parking space, jousting with the fogies. If only a
little of Jimmy rubbed off on me, he thought; if only we
could swap places for a while. Maybe Jimmy could
survive Scotland and Mother and Dad . . . ?

'Have you got a cigarette?'

The voice from nowhere was English yet alien. York-
shire, Lancashire? He swung round and saw the girl, a
long rangy girl with wild dark hair. Her eyes were huge
dishes. She was seated on a bench, her knees drawn
ungraciously up under her chin.

'I don't smoke,' he said but when he found the depths
of her eyes he saw a plea beyond cigarettes.

'Are you OK?'

'I don't know.' She looked away down the platform
at the departing express. 'Of course I'm OK, yes.'

Chas moved on across the concourse, then side-
stepped to a sales kiosk. He took a *Financial Times* and
a packet of Silk Cut. He walked back to the solitary girl
and stood clearing his throat ten feet from her. She
swung back to him with a puckered baby look that lifted
his heart. Her clothes, he saw, were rough and ready,
the jeans a size too big. She sucked a long strand of
brown hair.

'Here, your cigarettes.'

She looked at the pack, looking at his shining shoes.
'I don't smoke.'

'You don't smoke!'

'I'm sorry. I just wanted to talk to someone.'

He sent her a broad, smiling double-take, then sat
boldly alongside her. 'Are you going somewhere?' he
asked. 'And will this be a trick answer?'

She grinned in a sad sigh. 'I came down from the
north.'

'And where are you going?'

There was a long airy pause, then she sucked a new strand of hair. 'I dunno. I left home. At ten last night. My mother went to work and, well, I just walked out.'

'What's your name?'

'Louise.'

'Why did you leave?'

She sighed again, but this time with a kind of tight fury. Her face toughened and for a moment she was older than her teen years and almost dangerous-looking.

He stood up. 'Well, I'd better get my ass in gear, as they say in parliament.'

'I'll come with you.'

He laughed again, but Louise wasn't laughing. In fact, it crossed his mind, she wasn't far from crying. Her eyes were crooked and begging.

'Have you had breakfast?' he asked.

'Nope.'

'Neither have I.'

TWO

'Tis Woman, Woman Rules the Man

Some banks slumber. Some banks sing. Shane Long-man sang. Almost perpetually, a ringing choral symphony to Money, Midas, Man's Destiny. Leonard Ansen pushed the glass swing door and went through to the trading floor, a maze of octagonal screens to shoulder level. The music of a computer universe engulfed him: the piping teletypes, the bass Dow Jones, the counterpoint Reuters. Normally it lifted him. Today, marginally, it frightened him. This fear was good, it was primitive, a first cousin to jungle instinct.

First focus was Tokyo, where the market had been alive for the last ten hours. Leonard looked round urgently for Wendy, didn't see her, pegged Hannah. Hannah was bleary and sweating and he was tempted to voice concern; instead he asked about Tokyo. 'The Nikkei Index closed up fifty. There will be lots of buying today and we've a lot to sell. It looks fine.'

'You say that every day,' he frowned. 'Wendy?'

'Lee Wolf has her.'

'Shit.' He glanced at the weekend reports that had been burning him. 'Sirkka and Max?'

'Sirkka's just off the New York red-eye. She's at her station. I haven't seen Max.'

'Find him, fast.'

At the Secondary Markets desk, the selling desk, Sirkka was chewing a ham roll and cross-referencing equities, currencies, mortgages and bonds on her four-terminal system. The screens in her station danced with bar graphs and self-correcting analyses charts, the squawk box under her elbow barked sell-sell-sell appeals, the mood was early but electric. She threw down the sandwich and lit a Gaullois. When she saw Ansen she tapped out a second cigarette and offered, beads of peace. Leonard Ansen took in her sharp Finnish profile, her tight blonde locks, and knew again he couldn't be angry with her. Sirkka was headstrong but sound, a solid industrious woman who had worked as an agronomist for the UN, discharged herself with honour in Africa and the Middle East, drifted from land management to Eurobonds and never looked back. She was twenty-eight, mature beyond her years and yet volatile in a way few Finns are. She knew her own weakness and blamed it on her love life: her boyfriend, also a trader, was based in Copenhagen; their relationship was geographically unsound.

'You look terrible,' Ansen said straight.

'I feel worse. I managed to re-route to Copenhagen to see Sven – ' She tightened, watching him. 'You don't look all that hot.'

He slapped the weekend sheet. 'What the hell are you doing holding forty million Dodo notes? The way the market's going these will be garbage.'

'I'm not holding them. I . . .' she staggered, '. . . sold?'

'No you didn't, sweetheart. They're sitting there like snowballs in hell, all ready to roast.'

She was flustered. She turned away from him and banged her fist on the squawk box. 'Chas!'

'Tell me.'

'My fault.'

'Tell me, Sirkka. One of Wendy's boys gone soft again?'

She crushed the cigarette out, no joy in confessional betrayal. 'That crazy stupid kid. We discussed this. I told him to offload fast. I thought he'd traded with Chase.'

'Well, he hasn't been listening, has he? And let me tell you where you stand. We have US trade deficits at one thirty. I hope you're a serious gambling woman because the word is they'll be b-a-d – '

'Someone gave me a prediction of six point two or three billion, a considerable upswing – '

He shook his head aggressively. 'And we'll believe in fairies too! Come on, sweetheart, the market's going down the pan.' He stooped and whispered viciously. 'Get that soapy idiot in here and tan him. Sell. Everything. Before one thirty. Is that clear?'

'I'll do my best, Leonard.'

'Not your best, Sirkka. Do *it*. Sell.'

Not fear but gloom pumped through Ansen's system as he moved to stalk Max Lubin, whose nickname was 'The Alchemist'. Lubin, like so many, was Wendy's choice, an intellectual-cum-linguist who stumbled into banking and invented his own sub-department as Director of Swaps at the Capital Markets desk. Max's speciality was all things oriental – he had attended Peking University and had eleven Chinese dialects in addition to his seven European languages – and from this speciality grew an intricately tailored banking grand-plan involving Third Word Debt refinancing, based on high-risk swaps. Max Lubin was a famous – some said infamous – 'last resort'. His were always the maniac chances, the highest odds. And yet, on more than several occasions over the two years of his employment at Shane Longman, his were the greatest victories. No one sought out The Alchemist for idle words or amusement; one allowed him simply to get on with it – until there was a crisis.

Ansen found Max Lubin combing his stylish pigtail and generally prinking himself, serenading his reflection in the dead Reuters screen. 'Max?'

'Take it easy, old boy, I was on my way. Must make an effort to shine, you know.'

'Shine here.' Ansen shook the weekend sheet. 'It's a mess. The figures are yawning. I need something good. What can you do for me?'

Max Lubin's grey fox eyes sank deep into Ansen's. 'You think I'm insane, Leonard, don't you?'

'I do. But then it's a wild world. Lions growl because they have to.'

'Correct. And they're not an endangered species, if you get my meaning.' His brow furrowed deep. 'How bad?' This was something beyond bad quarterlies, Max knew; but he knew too that Leonard Ansen would play it tight and proud.

'I need ingenuity as well as black ink. I need some deals.'

Max twirled his chair, clapped his hands and grabbed some telex signals. 'How about this? Fantastic debt for equity move. A client sitting on a stack of Chilean debt wants to buy into a carpet manufacturing plant. I find another guy who's sitting on Polish ten year notes. We swap the Chilean paper into Polish notes. The client gets into his carpet plant and the Polish guy gets into a copper mine at sixty per cent below the market price!'

Ansen laughed, 'You're full of crap, Max.'

'But it's precisely what you need, old boy. It's the wag that gets chins wagging. That's what has brought Shane Longman – in its Leonard Ansen incarnation – to splendour. Clients hear and they come.'

It was true, of course, and Max was shining, as usual. No blame at his door. Ansen touched his shoulder and grinned a grateful grin. 'I'm edgy because we're doing OK. I want to keep doing OK but I'm no longer so sure I'll be given the chance.'

Max cupped his hand over Ansen's. 'I smell it in the lift, I smell it in the corridors, old boy. Something not too rosy afoot and the reckoning is nigh.'

'Find me a deal, Max, that's all I ask.'

Wendy Foley waited. It was nine; she'd been waiting one hour. The primish secretary (American) called Mabel punctured another file, spat a clip in and peeked across her wire-frames. 'Any minute now, I'm sure.'

The intercom whistled. Wolf came on. 'Mabel, tell Wendy I can't do it. Later, OK?'

Mabel tittered, something from a Hitchcock movie. 'He's *so* bad. Perhaps you'd better go. We'll buzz you down. I'm sure it will be sometime this morning.'

Wendy took up her clammy file and moved towards the stout mahogany door. The intercom sounded again. 'Mabel, cancel that. Send her in.'

A bile-like rage filled Wendy's mouth. She didn't wait for the unctuous Mabel but flung herself at Wolf's door. She pushed through, expecting him to be alone, expecting him to be absorbed in manicure, or feeding the windowsill pigeons. But he wasn't alone. A tall nautical-looking gentleman was seated across from him, one elegant heel propped at the edge of Wolf's leather-top desk. Wendy looked twice before she recognized the man as Peter Longman, the last tenuous family link to what had been, one hundred and ten years ago, a family bank. Peter Longman was fifty-four, but twinkled like a child. He sprang to his feet – a non-executive to his fingertips – and bounced towards her. He took both her hands, gave a vigorous shake and kissed her blushing cheek. 'As soon as I heard Lee say Wendy I thought, Peter Pan. That's the way you always made me feel. Remember that end-of-term party? The oil merger? We danced in Trafalgar fountain.'

Wendy chuckled. 'No, Peter, we did not. You just *think* we did. We ended up in someone's house in Denham watching a home movie of someone dancing in the fountain.'

'Really? Am I so old that my memory's failing?'

'You look younger every year.'

Across the room Lee Wolf sported an uncomfortable mandarin grin. Wendy could not resist unsettling it. 'I'm sorry if I'm a shade below my normal J. M. Barrie but I'm here to be chastised.'

'Really? Well, I'm here on a social call but I should wait around for this.' He guffawed, coughed, sat down again. 'One of the great joys in life is having enough money to infiltrate the executive suite whenever one likes, on one's own terms. It always feels like school here. But my stock – how much do I own, Lee? – keeps me above it all.'

'You own thirty per cent, Peter.'

'Imagine that! But no one can count in millions, so it means nothing. Believe me, girl, that kind of money means nothing.'

'Except when you feel the need to carpet a portion of Micronesia?'

Peter Longman shot into paroxysms of glee. 'Yes, yes, of course you're right. I own that island. Incredibly wonderful place. I play at being Stevenson or Gauguin or Hemingway or somebody. I have two wives. Well, not really wives, you know. But very docile and amenable native girls. One is called Purple Orchid, would you believe. Gorgeous woman, I adore her . . .' He sensed Lee Wolf's dejection and veered away. 'Anyway, I spend more time on the ranch in Colorado these days. I like Arabians, you know. I breed them.'

'You're a very fortunate man.'

His gaze grew close and fond. 'Yes, Wendy, I am. I pray a lot and I count my blessings.' He turned to Lee Wolf. 'But you're having problems with Wendy?'

'We're having the gremlins, I told you, Peter. The word on the street – '

'I never was much impressed by the word in the wine bars and trattorias. I always believed that small men listen to small voices down on the street. Big men look to the heavens for their guidance.'

Wolf was now having difficulty looking directly at Peter Longman. He twiddled a biro and repeatedly wet his teeth with the tip of his tongue. He grimaced – or did he smile? 'The thing is, Peter – Wendy has a style. Wendy and Leonard Ansen. They make up a kind of a team, you know . . .'

'A vital team, Lee. They are the signature of Shane Longman. The Big Desk. The way we are perceived is through them'.

'What I'm saying is, their techniques are unusual, the people they trust are unusual, the risk is sometimes unrealistic.'

'I see. You blame these doddery figures on a team and a style?'

'It speaks for itself.'

'Just a minute, Lee,' Wendy felt the spiral rise but before the sparks cascaded Peter Longman was cutting smoothly through her words and patting her hand. 'Come to the National Gallery with me. They have Picasso's Women. I want to take them in before I catch my flight. I hate art galleries when I'm alone. Lee won't mind?'

Before Wendy had her words Peter Longman had steered her through the office door and was casting platitudes over his shoulder to a speechless Lee Wolf. In the Wilton corridor, away from Mabel, Peter Longman kissed her hand. 'Wasn't that painless?'

'Peter, I appreciate your offer, but – '

'Forget it. Picasso's Women only confuse me. Give me simple Purple Orchid any day. I saw you storming. I guessed what was coming, and it's a waste of time. Seems to me you need to be trading. The American figures are in at one thirty and you need a telephone in your hand. Yes or no?'

She wanted to hug him.

'Lee Wolf is a jumped-up punk with an Empire grudge. How he ever got on the board defies me,' he went on.

'A lot of people like him.'

'Which depresses me by the day. The world is changing. It's the United States of Europe and a global outlook and no more place for heart and individualism. My grandaddy believed in individuality. He believed the word integrity was meaningless unless there was one heart, one soul, one purpose. But it's not like that anymore. It's committees, and committee manipulators like Lee Wolf.'

'That's a very flawed argument if you want me to start it.'

He laughed. 'I wouldn't dream of encouraging you. He who fights with a woman of purpose fails. That will be the subtitle of my epitaph. All my life I have avoided women of purpose.' He winked, prodded her. 'Now get back to your gun turret and win. No Yank is going to upend my piggy bank. At least, not while I'm alive.'

As Wendy and Peter Longman took the downward lift Lee Wolf exited his office and met Ralph Goldring in the hall. Goldring was five foot two and rounded, Hardy to Wolf's Laurel.

'Longman,' Ralph Goldring said sourly. 'Couldn't have been worse timing.'

'He's not sticking round. He's here for a few days to buy horses, going to Dublin tomorrow. Anyway, it may work to our advantage. We've nothing to hide. Let's take them all on. What we're trying to do is rebuild a sound and conservative bank. Longman should be kissing our boots.'

'Yes he should.'

'Have you talked round? How do we stand?'

'Twelve executive directors, five clearly on our side.'

'Then it all boils down to James Farrell. We simply convince him.'

'Red figures are all we need.'

'I think we have them beat.'

The phone in the men's room rang and Ted the attendant answered. A voice said, 'Is Jimmy Destry in there?' and when Ted said yes the phone went dead. Two minutes later Declan McConnochie slunk in, told Ted to find some coffee and parked outside the door of the one cubicle in use. A couple of minutes later Jimmy barrelled out and Declan hit him like a sidewinder. Jimmy crashed against the urinals, pirouetted like an ace and corrected himself. Before he blinked he *knew* what had hit him. 'Be sensible, Declan, for God's sake!' and he squatted into a defensive judo stance. Declan stood half a foot taller than him and two stone heavier: it was no contest.

'No one's ever done that to me, Jimmy. Just so as your book can balance at the end of the month, eh?'

'That's not the way it was, squire. You got it all wrong.'

'Put me right. The bonds sit in my name and it's going to cost me seven hundred and fifty thousand dollars. They're useless – '

'Who said useless?'

'I said. The penny dropped on Friday, when I heard exactly what Yamamoto Steel means on the market. I should have known better. I tried to get you Friday, and Saturday. And Sunday. You see, the trouble is, my book is bad. I've had a bad run where the coupons didn't fit. And that makes Wendy and Leonard Ansen quite sore – '

'Lewis will move them in Tokyo – '

'I tried him, Jimmy. He says no way. He says only a serious ass would trade in Yamamoto. And only a serious ass would cover for anyone who did. I'm that ass, Jimmy, and I don't like it. So it's the end of the line – '

Jimmy was suddenly bold and defiant. 'So what are you going to do, Declan? Tell Wendy I swung you one? That should make you look good.'

'You little bastard.' Declan lurched and took him by the Turnbull and Asser collar. 'It's not what I'm going to do. It's you, sunshine. You are about to try for a decent day's work for a change. You're going to earn your living. You are going to legally and ingeniously dispose of this muck, somewhere. Otherwise – '

'There's no otherwise.'

Declan sucked a breath and calmed down. He loosened his fist. 'Well, you have the advantage of vision, my son. You are quite right. There is no option. We're deep in this one together. I take it Wendy called you up about the second quarterlies?' Jimmy nodded. 'And we both know Wendy well enough to know that's a kind of penultimate twitch?' Jimmy nodded again. Declan put his nose close to the impish, smart-eyed dealer: the smell of Bond Street lotion drove him back. 'You have twenty-four hours, Jimmy. And if I lose my ticket because of you I'll see to it some way that you never work in the street again. And that's just desserts.'

'Screw you, big boy. You can ask, but you can't command – '

Declan was close to the point of poleaxing the sneering Jimmy when Hudson Talbot came in. As Declan recoiled Jimmy saw his chance and fled. Declan went to the basin and washed his face. He looked in the mirror – these days he was always looking in mirrors, looking for answers – but the face he found alarmed him. He spoke vaguely, half-addressing Hudson Talbot behind him. ' "Tis woman, woman rules the man." The poet Thomas Moore said that. How true it is. You know I'm twenty-nine. I first fell in love with a lady when I was fourteen. On the banks of the Avon, during a school outing, very tragic and perfect. When I was twenty I kept a score book. But the older I get, the lesser the passion. I've come to believe that a man has a capacity, a Plimsoll line . . .' He heard his own braggart wisdom, cloying, exaggerated, and he hated himself. 'I don't know. That, or maybe you just meet the right woman. Suddenly there's three sexes. Man, woman –

and *her*. You know what I mean? Have you ever met a lady who hit you like Frank Bruno – ?' He was rambling blithely and then, in a flash, he was aware that Hudson was ominously silent, his back still turned. 'Are you all right, Hudson?'

'Sure.' Hudson came to the basin and quickly splashed water in his face. He looked pink and jaded. 'I got a kid. A terrific eight-month-old kid who looks at me and smiles and I get a high like a ferris wheel. You can't beat that, Declan.'

'I suppose not.'

'In the meantime my advice – and bear in mind this comes from a married man – is, rub out that Plimsoll. Have fun.'

'Right.' It wasn't the advice Declan wanted, but this wasn't the conversation Hudson wanted. Declan saw this and he side-stepped. 'Can I ask some serious advice? Yamamoto Steel?'

'Wrong timing. Without the equity participation no one will want to touch it.'

'I guessed.'

Declan left the men's room in Poesque despair and steered to the farthest station where a scruffy lovely girl with a storm of dark blonde hair and a German accent shouted down a telephone. He fixed her in his gaze at a hundred paces and his eyes never shifted. She was his magic and his pain, she was Michelle Hauptmann.

Declan couldn't resist her bum. He patted its offered crescent. She jumped. Another phone shrilled, she snatched it up. 'Yes – what? – yes – all right – yes – he's here.' She pushed the receiver into Declan's nose. '*You*' – like he was some animal.

Declan said a cautious, 'Yes, McConnochie?'

'It's Wendy. At my desk. Get down here. I have Leonard Ansen.'

Declan dropped the phone. Michelle was twitching and shuffling like a weathervane and he held her arm. 'I'm sorry.'

'You always creep up, Declan. There are rules of exchange, you know.' He watched her, thinking, she tries to be mad at me and she never pulls it off. I amuse her; she likes me; maybe she loves me? He watched her mouth, the tugging underlip that belonged to a baby, never a twenty-four year old. He knew its touch on his cheek, never on the lips. Funny, she was probably the only female on the trading floor – teamakers included – whom he'd not kissed; not that there weren't opportunities; but the doing never seemed right, they were too close, too good friends.

'What's your trouble? That's the way it works, isn't it? When in trouble, you come to my door.'

'That's nonsense, Michelle. I value you highly, you know it.'

'I'm a junior trader, what would I know?'

'Why do you do that to yourself? The *junior* bit? It's this evasive thing that you keep on doing. Like living in the hotel. You're more than a year here and you're still in the same hotel Shane Longman put you in on day one. If you pitched Leonard Ansen – ?'

'Who says I'm staying here? I miss Frankfurt. I came on an orientation programme – '

'Rubbish. You're a cog. You're in. Wendy adores you – '

'But I like my space, Declan. I've applied for New York.'

It hit him low, in the solar plexus, and caused an audible pufffff. Inside, churning, he told himself to steady on, act his age. It was the old story of wanting what appears to be denied. If he kissed her once it would be fine: she would become just another moll, just a notch, a night. He tried to shrug. 'New York is over-populated. People go there from the City to bury themselves. It's a criminal hideout.'

'I'll write and tell you.'

'You can't be serious about this?'

She looked into his eyes and he sensed the unspoken words, the restrained welter that always confused him – and these days upset him. 'Tell me how I can help you, Declan?'

He told her: about the ten year notes he'd held for Jimmy and his dicey book. Wendy was under pressure, he had to get out. She listened with passion and thought a while, chewing her thumb. Her hair was lovely, lovely. 'There are two chances and I know Jimmy is already trying one, because he told me: Julie Iovine and Stephanie Keys. Jimmy is lunching Stephanie Keys.'

Declan knew the name, number and formidable image. He shook his head. 'Too academic for me. I don't understand her market. And I'm not sure Jimmy will – '

'So you'd prefer to leave your chances with Jimmy?'

He didn't need to review that. 'I'd prefer Julie Iovine. You worked for her at Citibank. So you know – ?'

'I know that Stephanie Keys is taking a lot of steel and I know that she likes a charming host. A charming *young* host. I can recommend you.'

Was she saying what he thought she was saying? Worst thing about love, Declan reflected; it mixes the wires. You find that elusive special *lingua franca* and you lose it and your days and evenings are full of that obsessive eternal quest; the mind boggles in overdrive. 'I don't want to sleep with some hag to discharge my debts!'

'Who said anything about sleeping with her!' Michelle

was horrified. She scraped her hair behind her ears and suddenly was sullen. 'I think you should stick to Julie Iovine. She's undependable, much more your league, Declan.' Her number one phone line went again and she grabbed it, and passed it to Declan. 'Yours.'

'I'll count to ten,' Wendy said gravely, and she meant it.

Chas Ewell scurried to his desk, head down, like a mouse. He took his swivel, loosened his tie and flicked the squawk box. Sirkka heard him and wheeled round the corner. 'Was it a woman?' she snapped, joking without humour.

'No, just got hung up.' He reddened, covered his blush. The girl had been full of surprises, not all of them comforting. Was he crazy to take her back to the house he shared with Jimmy in Islington? The box room was empty – in fact, half the house was empty – and it seemed churlish *not* to help. She was delighted, putting up firerockets. She hugged him in gratitude. She was child, she was woman. How old *was* she? Nineteen? or sixteen? He cringed. Those three years were a scary universe, beyond even Einstein.

'Wendy wants you, Leonard wants you – '

'What *is* this!'

'The quarterlies are dramatically bad and you sank me. I gave you all the information from database, I gave you my instruction – ' She keyed her terminal and the rundown of the disputed bonds flashed on screen. 'I thought you'd traded with Chase, like I asked.'

Chas's jaw fell as he saw the bond profile. 'No,' he muttered.

'I called you from New York. I said I wanted out.'

'Sure. But we agreed we'd hold off till the market traded up. We agreed to wait.'

'We agreed to sell.'

Wendy Foley's perfume made them turn. She looked stressed, with white blotches showing through her make-up. Her ears were up and she had heard Chas's contradiction. 'Well?' she directed Chas.

'I – ' Shirkka was top cat at Secondary Markets, but she had little vanity and no arrogance; most times, Chas thought, she tried too hard; unlike the other Secondary man-at-the-top Declan McConnochie, who tried too little. Chas liked Sirkka. She was a woman he looked up to, who played no games. 'I suppose I made a mistake.'

'Of course you made a mistake,' Sirkka rapped. 'And the way it stands, with the US trade figures coming, we have about three hours to clear this position.'

'Everything?'

'You bet your sweet ass,' Wendy said. 'All forty million.'

As Chas grabbed two phones and started dialling Sirkka tagged Wendy and touched her sleeve. She found it hard to hold Wendy's eyes. 'I don't want to interfere but I'd like to let you know that everyone on the floor is sympathetic. The talk in the restaurant – '

'Bad as that, is it?'

'I think if you lobbied round you'd find that everyone's on Leonard Ansen's side.'

'But that's not how the machinery works, Sirkka. The executives are a breed apart.'

'If we can help – '

'You can help by clearing up the red ink.'

Already Chas was cannoning: 'Hi, Jack! Chas at Shane. Listen, sell your nine and a half's. Buy Euro's. Nine eight's of ninety-three. It's an all-time winner, trust me.'

As Wendy listened and smiled Chas covered his mouthpiece and gave a thumbs up. 'Five million gone already. Just watch me.'

'Attaboy,' Wendy waved, and then she moved tiredly towards the kitchen to catch some caffeine.

In the kitchen she was surprised to find Leonard Ansen, an irregular visitor, filtering his sixth cup of coffee of the day, spooning it as strong as he could bear. He didn't look at her. 'I'm here to find out how the team's doing.'

'You tell me. Chas Ewell's selling the bonds fast.'

'Hudson's rechecking all our notes, doing what he does best. He'll advise on what to move fast. McConnochie's promising to respond to your tongue-lashing.' He sipped his coffee, and then passed a cup to her. 'Are we in the right game? Short nights, long days, other people's money. Intelligent people eat and sleep and watch TV. All we watch are those damn database readouts.'

Max entered, wide-eyed on seeing Ansen. 'Now I know there's a crisis! The situation is desperate indeed when the gods come from on high to sip with us.'

Wendy took the cue, gathered her papers. 'You console him, Max. Tell him we're better than we are. Give him hope.' She finished her coffee and left.

'Great girl,' Max said.

'Give me a deal, Max.'

'You got it. A great deal that'll make you rich.'

'And bump up the quarterlies?'

Max looked sad. 'No luck on that score yet. This is a different gen, Leonard. You told me last week you'd asked your broker to position some capital for you, after you sold your apartment building? Well look no further. Vellor and Marks is the deal. Lots of people – serious people – taking an interest in their stock. Trust an old salt: go for it.'

'I might need that capital, the way things are looking.'

'Good, then *go, go, go!*'

Leonard Ansen stood at the glass that gave a panoramic view of the trading floor. The bank of wall clocks opposite said: London 11.00 – New York 6.30 – Tokyo 20.30. The digital counters slipped as he watched, hurrying the countdown. His eyes raked the floor and he saw McConnochie haggling on the phone and Hudson Talbot fiddling with his computer and Chas Ewell laughing. He saw, but he took nothing in.

THREE

Casualties

The gym in the executive floor annexe was heavily stocked with the best Nautilus but infrequently used. It amused James Farrell, the bank's CEO, to reflect on its genesis. The petitions, the demands, the ultimatums. This was the Day of the Id, when all the fundamental instincts and energies of man must be catered for first. He must have the nutrition, he must have the exercise, he must have the room to be and to grow. So the gym went in, with round-the-clock access for all staff, and then no one came. James Farrell came, at first out of a prickly sense of duty (after all, it was his casting vote which granted it), and then because he liked it, liked the pain-gain stress that counterbalanced the boardroom. Once a week an instructor visited, to write up 'personal programmes', and Farrell followed his joyously, noting the widening bulk of his quads, the new flexibility of joints, at last the *hint* of washboards under the flab.

James Farrell was fifty-seven and battleworn. For-

merly Shane Longman's Director of Corporate Finance
– the job Lee Wolf now held – he had worked under
Ralph Longman, the last executive-active family
member, and survived a thousand changes in the company profile. When Longman died eighteen years ago
he had provided for Farrell in his will, ensuring an
upward-moving career and the inevitable role of chief
executive. But this heritage had its serious downside, it
was no pleasant canter. Farrell had fought with everything other than bare knuckles to see that Ralph Longman's hopes were realized. The years were exhausting,
and crushed two marriages, but at least he was still here
and still standing – and now there was the discipline of
the gym to build up the warrior in him and help him
stay on course.

James Farrell was thinking these bright thoughts
when he entered the gym at midday, but the mood
didn't last. At twelve fifteen, working the laterals
machine and struggling through an agonizing stitch,
the voice he least wanted to hear was piping in his ear.

'You OK, James?'

He looked under his arm at the upside-down face of
Lee Wolf, thinking, *no, not now*; and if it had to be
anyone, let it be anyone but Lee Wolf. To this day James
Farrell was confused as to how he had ever approved
the appointment of Wolf. Wolf was wolf by name and
nature. Not just his uncouth, uncompromising Amer-
icanism, but there was a hunger about him, a deadly
hunger. On a raft in a shipwreck you would never turn
your back on this man.

'I'm fine . . . a stitch . . . fine.'

'Here, let me help you. You look white, man. Are
you sure – ?'

'I said . . . fine.' Farrell heard his anger. He shuffled
to a stool and reached for the fridge. He took a Diet

Coke and the pain waned – and came – and waned. 'I'm OK. The laterals blow me out, always. Do you know a man's muscle-growth potential is dead after thirty? But I'm getting it here, and here.' Even in his discomfort there was satisfaction in pumping muscle in front of the fat American, showing him *how*.

'I want to postpone tomorrow's monthly meeting, if that's all right,' Wolf cut in.

'To get the second quarterlies?'

Wolf listened hard to check the sarcasm in Farrell's tone.

'I'm ready to read your "New Profile" paper. Peter Longman will be interested as well – ' Farrell went on.

'I've no problem with that, in case you're thinking otherwise.'

'So it's just strategy, is it?'

Lee Wolf considered, and decided he was on thin ice. No point locking horns with this one: James Farrell had a knack for winning out *his* way. Wolf smiled, revealing carefully hand-made teeth. 'James, I have nothing to hide. "Strategy" sounds Machiavellian and nasty. I'm just energy-saving. The end books will say a lot more about Shane Longman's state of health than any interim paper. That's all I'm saying.'

The pain vanished, as suddenly as it had come. Farrell stood and stretched and came eyeball to eyeball with Wolf. 'Can I ask you something, Lee? Do you understand Shane?'

'That's a damn fool question coming after ten years. For one thing, I rebuilt Venture Capital, James. I *invented* Leveraged Buy-Outs – '

'But I don't want us to become unrealistic. We are not a major league player. We have respect throughout the square mile. That was the intention of the Longman family, that is what Ralph Longman charged me to achieve. We have seven hundred employees in three countries – '

'Spare me the history lesson, James.'

Farrell took a deep breath, and grinned. 'You're right. It's wasted on you.'

'I have Shane Longman's interests at heart in everything I do. The whole planet is about evolution, growth. The dinosaurs have to move on, James.'

'And I'm a dinosaur, Lee?'

'No, not at all. That's not what I'm saying. But maybe Leonard Ansen *is*. Pioneering days call for mavericks, I agree. Leonard and Wendy Foley and that gang, they did what they were called in to do. They got us to first base – '

'Easy does it, Lee.' Farrell grabbed his kit bag and towel and headed for the showers. 'You're revealing too much of your hand. If this were a card game – '

Lee Wolf's fingers gripped Farrell's arm. Farrell turned and looked into a calm and confident gaze. 'This isn't a game, James. I'll say it again. I have nothing to hide. I'm not *playing*. I'm working. The facts stand: if we are not earning money, we are dying. And we are dying. And I'll tell you something else. Six members of the board agree with me. This phase of Shane Longman is over. Ansen and Company have to go.'

A moment's fragile silence followed, both men zinging. 'You won't unseat me, Lee. I'll be here till I'm dead.'

'That suits me fine, James.' He smiled. 'So what about the postponement of a meeting?'

'Sure, if you like. I'll take my chances on Ansen's team. My guess is they'll turn in some figures that will take the steam out of your paper.'

'You have great faith.'

'Yes,' James Farrell said, 'I do.'

*

At twelve thirty Jimmy Destry returned from an early lunch, upended a chair or two and flung his telephone into his Reuters screen. Everyone ducked, dived and sidestepped – except Hannah and Declan.

Hannah admonished, but Declan understood. 'Another blow out?' he asked bitterly.

Jimmy spoke through bared teeth. 'Stephanie Keys. I took her to lunch, if you could call it lunch – '

Declan shook his head. 'When will you ever learn, kid? Stephanie Keys is a little outside your league. She ate you up, right?'

'I didn't even get a hearing. I mentioned the notes and she threw me out! We barely touched the food!'

Declan clucked but held his patience. The ball was firmly in his court, there was no surprise in that. His phone purred and he snatched it. 'Mr McConky?' He tensed: this was *his* offload chance.

' – Connochie.'

'Yes, Miss Iovine will see you. For dinner.'

'I said lunch.'

'She finds lunch inconvenient. Dinner. Inn on the Park. Eight.'

Max swept into the vacant seat beside Declan. He looked flustered and his pigtail was crookedly ribboned. 'Do you have a fact sheet on Hungary?'

Declan was not feeling generous. 'Oh sure. Keep it here by my heart all the time. Prospects and Problems; The Cultural Milieu; The Health and Welfare Service Deficits. I mean, Hungary is where it's at!'

'Not today, Declan. My Chilean debts man has gone all funny. Wants to buy back Chilean debts and move into Hungarian steel.' Max cursed violently. 'I detest people who change their minds. Worse. I loath to death *clients* who change their minds.'

He was on his feet, whistling for Sirkka and her Hungarian expertise, but Declan held him. 'Max, you know about women.'

'Everything. Only trouble is, I've never been able to figure a way of making a legitimate living from my expertise. Unless I became an agony aunt, I suppose.'

'No, I mean City women. Julie Iovine.'

'A time waster. She'll dance rings round you. If you want to pitch a big buyer try Jimmy's tack, that broad Stephanie Keys.' He hesitated, swung back. 'Then again, leave her out.'

'Why?'

'Because she's a very earnest carnivore. She has a hit record to maintain and she refuses to lose. Ever. Which spells trouble if you're tinkering with a few odd bonds that stick in your craw.'

'I don't have the luxury of choice just now.'

'Want to tell me about it?'

'No time.'

It was twelve forty, with just fifty minutes till the American trade figures. The deadline pressed Declan, but not like it pressed Chas Ewell. Fifty yards away, at his station, Chas was thundering. Even Sirkka stepped back in respect, marvelling at his faultless selling, a bursting coil of pent-up energy. Wendy craned down: 'How's he moving?'

'He just sold Manny Hanny. Another five million. You have to give it to the kid.'

'Will he clear?'

'He might. If he stays alive.'

'Good boy. If he does it we have our first minor victory of the quarterlies.'

'You reckon the American figures will be down?'

'I reckon we'll be surprised by them.'

Sirkka looked close into the grey, tired eyes and frowned concern. 'Wendy, why don't you catch a bite of lunch and a glass of wine? You look like you could use it.'

'It's not a bad idea. Fortify myself for one thirty.'

Wendy moved towards the exit, toying with the referee's whistle she wore on a cord round her neck. It came in useful for stilling the floor, when she needed the attention of a far distant station. And it came in useful for summoning taxis. Maybe she would cab it up to her favourite haunt in Soho, take a long and radical lunch to wash away Howard and last night and the tensions of today? She laughed at herself. She would cross the fifty paces to the nearest eaterie as she always did, and hack the fastest lunch in town. The food didn't matter, the wine was of no consequence, but the fresh air and change of climate would bring her back to balance.

In the hall as she quit the lift a ruddy-faced gentleman with a broad raucous voice threw his arms out to greet her. 'Leaving the sinking ship?' he boomed.

'Is it *that* obvious?' she laughed.

It was Hal Lowenstein, one of Leonard Ansen's favoured lunch-and-golf companions, a gentle giant. 'Not married Leonard yet?' he persisted.

'It'd only end in tears, Hal. They'd never allow us to set up house on the trading floor. And who would cook, for heaven's sake?'

He roared his stentorian laughter. 'It's a point, I'll grant you. But, *if only!*' He squeezed her arm. 'I worry about Leonard. I'm like his big brother, you know. I want to see him succeed. He deserves the best. He has talent.'

'I know.'

Lowenstein's smile faded and his tone became serious. 'I know you know. You respect him and he repays you in kind. He trusts you, Wendy. You are his right arm.'

Wendy chatted some more and bade adieu as Lowenstein mounted the lift to rendezvous with Ansen for a promised lunch. As she left the bank her thoughts were full of Lowenstein's words. On any other day they would be gorgeous flattery. Today they felt like hell.

'Progress?'

Sirkka, Hannah and Max Lubin were corralled at the edge of Max's station, mouths agape, staring with admiration and awe at Chas Ewell scorching up the lines. None of them heard Wendy's question. Chas's shirt was three quarters open, his hair was matted with sweat, his face shining. He was juggling three phones and punching up Reuters as fast as his hands would work.

'I can't stand the tension. Are we winning or not?' Wendy insisted.

'He's got rid of thirty million. I heard him beg.' Sirkka's voice flooded towards tears. 'If ever a kid deserved his book, it's him.'

'He needs to get rid of it all.'

The London clock accelerated towards one twenty-seven. Just three minutes before the American trades – and the market swing, whichever way. Chas had dropped all but one phone now and as they watched he talked in tongues. 'Larry, five year Euro's are boss, man. Call it a junior tip, given in innocence. Give me faith, man. I'll take Lomo stock to Swaps, I'll make it work for you . . .'

'He won't make it,' Max murmured.

A minute to go. Fifty seconds. Forty seconds. He was still pleading, still down. 'How's your kid, Larry?' He side-glanced and saw the knot of anxious faces waiting. He paled, swivelled his chair away. 'Great, Larry. Yes, we'll have a drink. Sail? No I haven't sailed. I'd like that. Sure, I'll crew for you. Plenty of muscle. Now about the bond . . . ?' Twenty seconds . . .

And all of a sudden he was spinning his chair, beating his heels, tearing his hair. The phone was dashed aside. He let out a yell. *'Got it!* Square. Forty million!'

'Good boy!' Wendy hugged him. Sirkka pushed up the squawk box at her station. 'Watch this market go down!' Wendy said, but Sirkka wasn't so confident. The megaweight tiredness of a couple of weeks of endless travel, last night's long flight, a thousand forgotten dealer tips in twenty countries – all of it came crashing down, pricking the carnival balloon. Why was she hesitant? Why did this victory feel like defeat? Why did she feel – of all things – guilty?

The squawk box sounded: 'The US second quarter trade deficit reports at six point three billion, continuing to indicate a month on month improvement . . .'

'It's what I said,' Sirkka mumbled, aghast. 'An improvement.' She shuddered in shame and Chas was staring at her, his face ashen. The pencil he held snapped in his hands. Sirkka turned away as Wendy turned away and the words rolled out, mocking them: '. . . . Market responds favourably . . . Gilts, Treasury showing an upswing . . .'

'We blew it,' Wendy gasped. 'Our biggest, simplest chance and we blew it.' She looked at Chas. 'You ran this position the wrong way, kid. You should have held onto all this stuff – '

Chas stood up, buttoned his shirt and walked towards the kitchen. He showed no expression.

'We could have made a killing,' Max said. 'But what's the point in crying over spilt milk?' He looked at Sirkka.

'You and Leonard agreed you had to offload, right? No shame in that. Pros make their decision and act it out. You win some, you lose some.'

'Not this time,' Wendy said. 'Not this time.'

Sirkka could not bear the brunt of Wendy's upset. She left the station and followed Chas Ewell into the kitchen. The dealing floor was whirling into action, the din intolerable. Sirkka closed the door tight, shutting out the noise. Chas was bathing his face with a wet handkerchief. He smiled at her lifelessly. 'Nothing I can say will make it any easier for you,' he said.

'We agreed to wait, not sell?'

'That's it. I didn't want to contradict you. It seemed to me, once the Bank of Japan announced second quarter reduction in surplus, the US figures had to be better. I understood you went along with that – '

'I lost it.' She cursed and kicked the ground. 'I worked a plan and then I forgot it and when Leonard Ansen hit me I tumbled in a heap. That's bad, Chas. That's getting old and tired. That's quitting time.'

He came to her and held her tight. 'Tired maybe, never old. We did our best. No one can ask for any more.'

'We put them under,' Sirkka said. 'You know like I know. It's the end of the line, Chas.'

FOUR

Love
Is the
Big Risk

Squandering money, big money, takes a Declan McConnochie type of ingenuity. As he waited in the bar at the Inn on the Park Declan asked the barman to crack a vintage Rioja, and when that didn't suit his palate the restaurant sommelier was found and a '53 *Château La Conseillante*, the finest Pomerol Grand Cru, replaced it. That took care of a hundred and fifty quid – and still he had just a couple of glasses of alcohol in his belly and that tense, unsated feeling. He glanced at his Cartier wristwatch and told himself the current crisis was no different from all the others. But the reassurance rang hollow. When he had left the office at five the *silence* had been pronounced and extraordinary. There was something crypt-like about the corridors, no one talked much in the lifts. The bushfire rumours of earlier had died down: no one mentioned the cabals upstairs, or how devastating a shake-up might be. There was a sense of jaded completion, that a final chapter in yet another Shane phase was drawing to an irreversible close, that serious blood-spilling and victims were inevitable.

Declan swept back a big glass of the Bordeaux and told himself: keep a clear head, don't get distracted by other people's death rattles, save yourself – because you must. He looked again at his watch. Eight forty-five. No, he told himself, I will not succumb. I will stay hearty and keen. Positive thinking wins out all the time. Send out those Good, Good, Good Vibrations. The barman slid a phone under him: 'Miss Julie Iovine.'

His palms were wet. 'Hi, Julie – ?' Sounding like, 'HI, JULIE!'

The voice at the other end was flat, masculine. 'Hi, I'm sorry I can't make it – '

'Oh, why not?'

All apology faded from the voice, to be replaced by a stern irritation. 'I've just got something developing here. I can't leave it.'

'I understand. It's just that I hoped – '

'Sorry, definitely another time.'

Declan sat with the dead line and a dead-eyed barman gaping at him. The wine in his other hand was suddenly tacky and tasteless. His brain reeled, then steadied. An instinct drove him to his briefcase, parked on the seat beside him. He found his address book, blanked his mind to any flicker of doubt and dialled a number. It was a chance, a crazy chance – but why not? He was powdered, tanked and ready for a date. He wanted a woman to yap to, to parry with, to win. And he wanted a deal.

A lazy, sexy voice came down the phone. 'Yes? It's Stephanie.'

He talked fast, very fast, lest the courage went. 'Hi, Stephanie. We know each other by reputation, I guess.

Declan McConnochie from Shane. Someone brought up your name today – '

'What do you want?'

He tried to sound impressively good-natured. 'Here I am with a lot of time to kill, enjoying a superb Bordeaux and wondering if I could persuade you . . .' It sounded absurd, pathetic, but he kept on rolling.

She listened, and then there was a long, laboured silence. Did she laugh? Or was it his imagination. He waited for the line to cut off but instead she sighed and said, 'Do you know Tiberio's?'

'Sure I do. I can be there in – '

'I'll see you there at ten.'

Declan paid his bill and called a cab and was pushing through the glass door and moving down the tree-shaded steps of Tiberio's twenty minutes early. In situations like this, he told himself, it's best to switch to a low automatic gear. Buzz quietly and efficiently, don't zoom. Be punctual and obedient, give her room. Give her the secure feeling that she's the one calling all the shots. Give her rope enough . . .

But she was here before him, quietly seated in a shaded corner under a pot palm, chewing the edge of a serious drink. He looked twice. This was not the Stephanie Keys he expected. Her face was familiar from trade papers and from some function somewhere sometime – but that was a century ago. The woman he recalled was aquiline and hard. This vision in the corner was pouting, soft and classically Jewish. He loved the cut of her suit and the big Coco Chanel business on her wrist. Her eyes didn't smile, but marched over him like an army parade. She didn't shift her rump off the gilt chair.

'I'm sorry I dragged you out so late,' he heard himself grovel, 'but it seemed like a great idea. Spontaneity –

all that.' She didn't budge, didn't grin, didn't look left or right as he summoned a waiter.

'Menu, sir?' The waiter started, but Stephanie Keys shook her head. Her eyes bore into Declan's. 'Have a drink.'

'All right.' He smiled at the glowering waiter. 'Make it a glass of wine . . .' He reversed: 'No, whisky.'

The waiter fled and Stephanie hinted at a smile at last. 'Do you always start so serious?'

'Serious?'

'Whisky. Only gamblers, crooks and barristers go for whisky.'

'Really? That's interesting. And probably accurate. As a matter of fact I started out in the legal profession, but I flunked the final exam – '

'So you settled for being a crook?'

He laughed. Alone. He lit a rare cigarette, flashing his gold Dunhill, scrambling inwardly for a line that might measure up. 'As the great Lord Byron said – '

'I've eaten,' she cut in, no apologies.

'You've . . . eaten?'

'So let's get out of here. Have you got a car?'

'I have . . . *had*. They clamped me. Outrageous really. I parked up Chancery Lane, looking for a blurb from a pal in Fleet Street – '

'We'll get a cab.'

Declan managed to get the whisky down while Stephanie paid the bill and ordered her taxi. When it arrived she got in and he had the chance to admire her neat rear end. She instructed the driver, sat back and said, 'Do you like what you see?' Declan was obliged to ask her to repeat the question lest he had misheard. He wondered, was she drunk? But she smelled like a petal.

'I have a friend who owns a terrific apartment over-looking the river – ' he began.

'Let's not talk garbage,' she said. She laid back her head and closed her eyes.

Stephanie Keys's apartment was Arab rich. It was a glitz penthouse, with a long twinkling view of the Thames, Art Deco furniture and out-of-place Dutch paintings. The central lounge was fifty by fifty, with a central well whose walls were lined with hi-fi equipment and cushiony recesses. She placed Declan here – in a purposeful gesture akin to potting flowers – and went to the bathroom. When she returned she was dressed in cliché cosies, with bare feet. She sat opposite him and he was somehow relieved to see that her make-up was still in place. He hadn't been offered a drink and he felt naked without one.

'So tell me about Shane,' she said.

'Oh, it goes on, you know.' He laughed, squeezed his charm through a tightening bottleneck. 'Now and then it comes up rosy and we all do well. Like the present situation. Something quite good I've got that I thought you might like. I know Jimmy probably tried to explain. But he's a kid – '

'Do you want to go to bed?'

'I – I'm reasonably tired, yes.'

His wit was wasted. She just looked him over like he was an idiot and headed for the bedroom, switching down the lights. He found the bathroom and took off his tie and checked his teeth in the mirror. He found himself thinking ravingly about Michelle, about how she could do this to him. He remembered her growl when he said he didn't want to sleep with anyone to fix his book. It felt good that she'd reacted that way; it felt good because it felt like she cared.

In the bedroom Stephanie was already under the

covers, her rusty hair spread against the quilted satin headboard. For the first time she smiled and in its unexpectedness the smile was nerve-wracking. Declan fumbled out of his pants and slid into the kingsize arena. She smelled good, felt good, but when he touched her it was unreal and her kiss was dry and hard as untreated leather. Her caress was fierce, nearly painful, and her instructions many. He obeyed, working as well as he could, and it was all over in five minutes. He lay beside her in a trance, assuming she was replete and resting. Instead, she explained, 'I make a point of never spending the night with anyone. Would you mind . . . ?'

He was winded. 'I – I don't know what you mean?'

'I mean, goodbye.'

He gave a nervous boy's giggle. 'I came to talk to you – '

'I don't want to buy anything just now.'

'But you haven't even heard what I'm selling. Listen, there's some cheap ten year notes. They'll make ten points in three weeks. Three months down the road you'll see a hell of a return. The Japs love them – '

'What are they?'

'Yamamoto Steel.'

'Everyone's getting out of that shit. Without the equity it's nothing.'

'Listen, that's not true. These bonds are still attractive, dead attractive. They've got a low coupon, they're tax efficient – '

'You obviously love them, so keep them. I'm sorry, I really can't help. We're wasting each other's time.'

Declan felt his blood boil. 'This is very unfriendly, Stephanie – '

She jacked up in the bed and punched a fist into his chest. 'Who the hell do you think you are? It's open

season all year round in the square mile, I accept that.
So you made a pitch. Fine. I don't want it – '

'But you'll take whatever else is on offer, right?'

Her face darkened, became dangerous. Her nails
were long and she placed the fingernail of her index
finger just under his eye. 'I'm all grown up, lover boy,
and I know the way the world works. I beat you to it, so
who's counting, who cares? Don't tell me you weren't
prepared to go the distance, no matter if I looked like
Methuselah's mother, once you got your deal. So you
missed the deal. The woman hit checkmate first.'

'That's pathetic.' He pulled away from her and got
his clothes. He felt wounded, raped. 'I came to you
with a perfectly legitimate proposal – '

'Bullshit!' she chortled. 'The self-delusions of men! I
do homework, sonny. I know about you. You are small
fry. Shane Longman might be getting there, but it has
some way to go, never forget that.'

He dressed in the bathroom, so choked with anger
that he could not see himself in the mirror. As quickly
as he could he tidied himself and bolted for the exit.
She was leaning on the bedroom jamb when he opened
the hall door. 'Egyptian proverb,' she smiled. 'God be
between you and harm in all the empty places you
walk.'

The doorman at Michelle's hotel, a fat kid called Andy,
knew him well. Andy frequently benefited by Declan's
expertise at Doncaster, Cheltenham – all the good turf.
Without a word he waved Declan to the lift.

Michelle opened the door in a wrap. She saw the two
bottles of champagne and her spirits sank. But then she
looked into Declan's face. 'I have to be up at five,' she
said warily. 'But you'd better come in.'

The room was an hotel room, but it had Michelle's meticulous stamp all over it. Declan was relieved to be here, in hiding, light years removed from the disorganized blur of his own life. He wanted to run into her arms, to be home. 'I called back to my place and got a message on my machine. A death threat. Like to hear it?' He didn't wait for her response but ran it on her sound deck. It was Wendy Foley, in uniform, wearing her stripes and a frown:

'Declan, this is the call no one wants to get . . . or to give. I tried to get you at the office, but I was tied up. We're having a rocky ride and I think you know that. The major anomalies have got a little more, er, noticeable, in the last couple of hours. So I need more than reassurances. I need a deal. I'm sorry, but if you don't come through I have to initiate a response. Unfortunately I'm under a lot of pressure . . .' There was a pause, the sound of a glass tinkling, and then: 'Give me a deal tomorrow, OK?'

Michelle pulled down the corners of her mouth and plugged in the coffee-maker. 'Sounds like she means it,' she said.

'Great, that's what I came here to hear. Well done, Michelle – '

'Calm down, for heaven's sake – '

'Calm down! Calm down after what you threw me into! Stephanie Keys. Or should it be, Tease. That woman is an animal. A disgrace – '

'Wait a second, Declan. I didn't *throw you in*. You asked my advice on steel – '

'To teach me a lesson, was it? You think you know me. You think you know the way I am and you wanted to rub my nose in it – '

Michelle walked quietly to the door and opened it. The night time serenity of the hall yawned at him, hushing him. 'If you came to rant and scream you can leave. Now. I didn't ask you round. I never do, Declan. You invite yourself every time. But this is *my* home and despite my hospitality, *I* make the rules. Remember that.'

He sat in a heap on the settee and dragged his fingers through his hair. He addressed the carpet and his tone was apologetic; he was the little boy lost again, and she sighed inwardly. 'You turn me into pastry at times, Michelle, you really do. I feel about so high – '

'Someone's got to do it.' She returned to the coffee. 'Stephanie Keys turned you down?'

'Right after she chewed me and digested me and coughed me up and spat me out. She wanted a bedmate.'

'And you played ball?' She sat opposite him on a soft chair and handed him a steaming, fragrant mug. His eyes avoided hers and he drank the coffee fast. She went on in a sensitive, hurting voice: 'You are an idiot, Declan. You think with your penis at times. Someone's got to say that to you. Someone's got to tell you it's grown-up time – '

He bridled. 'You were the one – '

She shook her head and her eyes were big sad saucers. 'Stephanie Keys is big time, Declan. She makes a smooth living by pulling off coups. I thought maybe, just maybe, you were man enough to handle her. But you weren't. You're still in kindergarten. All you see is this battle of the sexes, this pillow game. If you live by the sword, Declan, you'll die by the sword.'

The sadness of her eyes scared him, he didn't want to know. 'I got clamped,' he hedged.

'Your car?'

'It really isn't my week. But God loves a fighter. So I got some bolt cutters – '

'You didn't break the clamp? Oh, Declan – ' She got up to fetch the coffee pot and he held her arm.

'You're not serious about New York?' he said. 'I couldn't bear it if I had no one to criticize me any more.'

'Will Wendy and Leonard Ansen not provide?'

'Maybe not. I could be out of a job tomorrow.'

The rushing sympathy of her eyes lifted him; but it always stopped short of the right words, the essential deeds. She pulled away. 'You'll think of something.'

'It isn't like you think it is, Michelle. It's just that I don't want to lose you – ' But there was no sympathy in her eyes now, just that cold Nordic stare. This was not the way he wanted it to be. This was not the home he dreamed of. On other nights, on less strange nights, they laughed through their misunderstandings. Tonight should have been a roaring log fire, and champagne, and cuddled-up comfort. Instead, this emptiness. What was happening to the world? What was happening to his legendary charm, his celebrated timing?

'I'd better go,' he said. 'It's nearly midnight and I suppose we're both running at dawn.' He fixed his tie and put the champagne neatly in the fridge and pecked her in his usual way, on her cheek. For a split second, as she closed the door on him, he thought he saw a moistness like tears in her eyes but he was tired, so tired, and he could have been wrong.

Riding the lift the numbing pulse of all-out exhaustion began, a throb that starts in the heart and floods the soul. Andy said something about Ascot to which he half-responded, and then he was pushing the swing door and finding the reviving night air. Collie and last night seemed an eternity away and yet they filled him entirely, reminding him of the futility of his energies, the wasteland that was his world. He heard a voice, a haunting distant voice, and it was Michelle, like

Heathcliff's Kathy, crying to him. What was she saying? What declarations of love, what promises, what lifelines?

'Declan – Declan, can you hear me?' And then a glass-splintering yell. He turned, looked up. She was hanging out of the window. 'Declan!'

'I thought I was hearing things! What's wrong?'

'An idea. About those notes. You said steel, yes?'

'Steel it is.'

'I know someone who's looking for steel. Max. His Chilean debts man wants into Hungarian steel – '

Of course! The client who changed his mind! The one Max loved to loath. Declan flicked his sleeve: 12.05. Knowing Max, he'd be bed-bound by now, with a book and a calculator and a plan to buy some obscure African township. With a bit of luck, his African ambitions would keep him awake a while yet . . .

'You're an angel. I love you!' He laughed aloud.

'I love you too.' She waved gaily and he ran with wings on his heels.

Max's split-level house was Beverly Hills-Bayswater but somehow unfunny. Like Max himself, the house had character and a fundamental seriousness. Declan parked on the Venetian-tiled drive in the space normally occupied by Max's prized Bristol, a car in a million. The Bristol's absence hinted that Max wasn't home, and yet a light burned in the den window. Declan took his loop of keys and selected the appropriate one. Among the cut-copies and skeletons on his loop were keys to Sirkka's, to Sophie, the kitchen manageress' – fond reflection of the dusty charm that once was. Many times he had 'crashed' his friends' apartments and houses, often on the run from a woman or a landlord, more often seeking solace after a bad day's trading. Max's he liked best – and least. The house was *too* spectacular, too much the gilded cage. Max's wild imagination had gone to town on the discordant decor so that ancient art contrasted blindingly with Gothic curiosities. Everywhere said 'Don't Touch', and this limitation alone quenched Declan's fun.

As he pressed the hall light switch a conspicuous blonde lady in a black leather stovepipe dress skipped a step in the middle of the floor and blinked at him. She raised the glass in her hand. 'Papaya juice,' she said in a stout French accent. 'Max keeps everyzing!'

'I'm sure he does.'

The woman grinned, handed her glass to Declan, kissed the tip of her witch-like finger and touched his mouth. 'Be a darling and remind me about the garage?'

Declan pointed. 'Thataway – '

'Chéri!'

The woman disappeared, witch-like. A Bahamian conch shell carved like a horn was too close to miss. Declan took it and hollered: *'Max?'*

In a second Max came whirling down the stairway, his tropical nightshirt billowing. 'Declan! A woman. Did you see a woman?'

'I don't know, Max. Describe her.'

'Seriously, Declan.'

They fell silent. Nearby a car engine boomed, and revved, and boomed away into the night. 'Good God, man! The Bristol! The bitch. I knew it. I set myself up. I met her in that snazzy laundromat. Dressed like that, I knew she was too good to be true.'

'Her clothes were in the spinners, right?'

'Something like that. *Hell!*'

'I sympathize, Max. It's a night for Jezebels. I just had Stephanie Keys. Do you want to call the police?'

While Max made phone calls and raved away in five languages Declan made up some earnest Martinis. His hands were shaking as he mixed and he stopped and sat on the high tubular bar stool and ran the events of the night quickly through his mind. He decided instantly that his whole world needed reassessment. He had made his reputation by sailing close to the wind, but too often now he sailed too close, and took too much for granted. He was sailing too close with Shane – and with Michelle. He wanted them. Maybe more; maybe *needed* them. The notion of loss was suddenly unbearable – as was reflection on the murk that was his present lifestyle. The faces of Collie and Stephanie Keys came, mockingly, and his stomach rolled over.

When Max came into the bar Declan jumped at him. 'I need The Alchemist, Max – '

'Declan, for the Lord's sake, I need some time off.'

'You know what happened today. You know how bad the word is from upstairs. Well let me tell you who's going to be the first log to fall. Me.'

'That figures.'

'Don't console me.'

'I won't.'

'I'm sitting on some ten year notes for Jimmy Destry – '

'And Jimmy can't unload them? And Jimmy's gone running for cover?'

'You're a detective, Max. You missed your calling.'

'And this explains your canoodling with the dangerous Miss Keys?'

'Jezebel.'

Max clucked and shook his head. He filled Declan's glass with vodka. 'You should have spilled it out to me, my son. You are too young for such byways – '

'Now I'll spill it out for you. I'm dead meat unless I sell today – '

'Illuminate me. What notes?'

'Three per cent. Ninety-eights. Yamamoto Steel.'

Max transformed from Mad Max, night time Max, to the Max people paid for. His face screwed into concentration, his troubles were forgotten. 'Yamamoto? Small Japanese company, isn't it? Part of Oriental Gulf, separated in '79, new MD last summer, moved administration to the States? Exploring off West Africa . . . ?'

'You got it. Sound good?'

'No, unless someone wants it.'

'Someone does. Your Chilean debts fellow maybe?'

The scowl vanished from Max's face and he snatched the phone from the bartop. He dialled a number, and waited. After a minute he put the phone down. 'He switches off the phone when he wants an early night. Hudson. I think we should talk to him for an evaluation. We may have a common objective, you and I. The coupon sounds good for tax . . .' Max was already fetching coat and hat. He pulled the fedora low over his eyes and killed the lights. 'Ready?'

'What about your car? The girl? The police – '

'Deal first,' he said.

In Declan's car driving to Highgate Max gave his evaluation of the power-play within Shane Longman. 'It a question of bottle,' he said. 'The stock exchange has changed, the market is free and wild and will get freer and wilder in the nineties. It's the Day of the Maverick and Leonard sees it, but Lee Wolf chooses not to. Wolf appeals to the old spirit, the spirit of a market that's dead and gone. But people are sentimental, even when money's involved. They like things left alone. They like things not to change. A lot of people are scared by Leonard and Wendy – and I suppose by me.

They see us as the Young Turks who rape markets and upset the order. That's what Leonard is fighting and the trouble is he's got to score big and significant to impress anyone that the change for Shane is worthwhile.'

'I should have thought he'd scored big enough already. The health of the bank today bears witness. James Farrell admits it. It was Leonard Ansen's direction-making that put the bank where it is.'

'People have short memories, Declan. After the Longmans the bank had its down period and then – yes – Leonard arrived and it recovered and redesigned itself. But the last couple of months have marked a heavy downward trend – '

'The market made that trend.'

'Sure. We can argue that all night long. People judge by banks and brokers. No one said there's forgiveness or understanding in the street. The point is, the failure is perceived by Lee to be Leonard's and Wendy's – and yours. So your "style" fails, and that's all there is to it. The real sad part is that you and I know that Shane Longman cannot thrive in its old format. James Farrell is good, but he's not far-sighted. He belongs to the twentieth century and now we're almost in the twenty-first century. If he gives in to Lee and Ralph and the others, my guess is the bank is finished. We're too little, or too inbetween.'

By the time they pulled up at Hudson's door in Highgate Declan's head was throbbing and his forehead was wet. This was his last chance; this *had* to work. All of a sudden Shane's future, not just his, was in the balance.

Max pushed the bell, but no one answered. 'There's plenty of lights on,' Declan said. 'And it's only half one. Doesn't he have a housekeeper?'

'You don't have a skeleton, I suppose?'

'Not this one – regrets.'

'I'll try round the back,' Max said. But suddenly the door opened and Hudson Talbot swayed in the hall light, bleary-faced and tying up his dressing gown. His pallor and the fuzzy, faraway look in his eyes instantly alarmed Max and Declan.

'Hey, guys,' he drawled, but the edge was gone, 'it's past one – '

'Are you OK, Hudson?'

He rubbed his eyes, grimaced. 'I've got a little problem. Alex has gone. I mean . . . *gone.*' His voice briefly wavered.

'Jesus, you're kidding! What about the baby?'

'I've got the baby. The baby's here with me.' He jerked his head inside. 'I suppose I must be . . . grateful.'

'How *is* Jamie?' Declan put in. 'Is he asleep?'

In answer, a blood-curdling wail echoed down the stairs and Hudson smiled exhaustedly. 'He *was* asleep. Doesn't matter, I had to feed him anyway – ' He frowned. 'If I can muster up the damn food. Domesticity isn't my bag, if you know what I mean.'

'What do you need?' Max offered with enthusiasm. 'Baby food? Desserts? Nappies? Gripe water? Give me ten minutes. There's an all-night shop round the corner . . .'

When Max had departed Hudson led Declan into the lounge and hurried upstairs to fetch the baby. On his return he pegged Declan about the reasons for this dead-of-night call but Declan was lost in the baby. 'What a cutie,' Declan cooed. 'I can't believe Alex would just toss him aside. Have you any idea where she is? It's inconceivable that she could just walk out!'

'Well she did. This morning we talked but today,

when I got back from the bank . . .' Again his voice
faltered. 'I don't know, I just don't know. She's been
acting so strange. I saw a problem coming and I tried
to divert it. I tried to get her to talk about it.' He rocked
the baby as the wailing recommenced. 'Seems to me it's
a conflict of interests. She won't admit it to me. Secretly
she wants to be something else, leading a different kind
of life.'

'I don't believe it. I'm sorry, Hudson. I don't know
her so well but I do know a little. I've seen how she
loves you, how good the two of your are together – '

The intimacy of the conversation embarrassed
Hudson. He turned his back on Declan and paced with
the weeping child. 'You don't know the other side of
her.'

'Does anyone know the flip side of anyone? It's a
theory I'm working on: that people have a hidden side.
Even you, Hudson. Maybe the problem's not her, it's
you.'

The sound of the doorbell broke the embarrassed
moment. Max was back with his booty: nappies, gripe
water, baby socks and all. 'I won't offer to feed the little
critter,' Max declared, 'but I'll be brave and watch.'

'You guys want to make yourselves more useful and
tell me why you're here?'

Max hung his head with guilty look. 'In the circumstances it seems out of place – '

'But not redundant,' Declan put in anxiously.

'I'm a big boy,' Hudson said. 'Me and Jamie'll be fine.
It's something we'll just have to work out ourselves.
Now, don't be polite, folks. You've done enough already.
Let's get this bottle made up in the kitchen, eh?'

In the kitchen Max spilled it out: 'We want a risk
evaluation on a conversion with a tax query.'

Hudson looked like he was about to start crying, but

he started to laugh. 'I'm not sure what's crazy anymore. It's halfway to dawn, my wife has left me, I'm not sure which way is up, the baby is . . . oh, for God's sake, Jamie, keep still . . . the baby is out of control, and my office buddies are looking for risk checks on debts-for-equities swaps and junk bonds and tax management.'

'Just one deal, Hudson. But it could save Declan's skin – and maybe Leonard Ansen's.'

Hudson slid the baby into a kitchen cradle and plugged him with a soother. As the kettle boiled he sighed, 'OK, let's hear it all.'

The explanations and discussions raged for a full half hour, during which time the baby was fed, washed and changed. When Hudson went upstairs to settle Jamie in his cot Max found himself staring aghast at Declan. 'Look at you,' Max said, 'I haven't seen a spookier face since my laundromat blonde. You're stone dead.'

'Dead tired. I've slept twenty minutes in two days.'

'No sense keeling over on the day you get the chop. Why not grab a few hours shut-eye here?'

'You're right. And someone had better stick with Hudson in the circumstances. If only to help change nappies.'

Hudson came into the kitchen with the ghost of a grin, for a moment almost looking like himself. 'There's a positive tax advantage for the Chilean debts man.'

'That's all I wanted to hear,' Max chirped. 'If you wouldn't mind, Hudson, perhaps Declan can intrude upon you for a decent night's sleep?' Hudson said sure. 'Then I can run over the details of this with you – now – and get on to Shane. I can be on the phone to Julio, my man, by nine.'

'Why am I doing this? Hudson asked, reaching for the coffee.

'Boredom,' Declan grinned.

In the silent, empty hall Declan's knees buckled, but he recovered himself and started on the stairs. On the landing a picture of Alex lay crumpled, discarded. He lifted it and looked into her face. For his own reasons, the unfathomable depths and heights, Hudson loved Alex. And in her way, Declan was in no doubt, Alex loved Hudson. The methods and meanings are always a mystery to onlookers. And love is the Big Risk, that's all.

At nine fifteen, Max put down the phone on Julio. The trading room was humming. He called across to Declan: 'The deal flies. Julio takes the swap. You're home and dry.'

'How's Wendy?'

'Crying.'

FIVE

Bad Weather

The rest of the week had a celebratory feel, like Christmas all over. Everyone seemed to feel it. The reception desk smiles were sunnier than usual, the charge on the trading floor was extra-high voltage. 'All because of my lousy deal,' Declan liked to brag, but of course it was more than that. Declan wasn't the only high hitter of the week, but he started the trend. By Friday Sirkka, Michelle and Chas had pulled notable deals and a palpable relaxation manifested itself. Sirkka walked in a dream, bumping furniture and telling anyone who'd listen, 'I think it might click, I think we might hold it,' and even Jimmy Destry made an appearance and shuffled some Eurobonds competently.

Wendy and Leonard Ansen – who had each spent a deskbound weekend stoking the Primary Market – met for breakfast in Ansen's office on Monday to review progress and professed themselves well pleased. 'I'm happy if you're happy,' Wendy told Ansen. 'The nicest thing is the way the floor has responded; the coming together of everyone without speech-making. I think you should be flattered.'

'You mean they do it for me and not for themselves?' His dark eyes twinkled mischievously.

'Sometimes.'

'I really must look into this Buddhism business. It makes good people great.' He frowned. 'Why can't I picture Jimmy Destry lying awake worrying about my executive status?'

She laughed. 'I said "sometimes". But what does it matter if the effect works?' She hesitated. 'They do care. Lots of them care very much – '

He was lost in the week's figures again, flipping pages and scowling. 'Capital Markets, Eurobonds – they're our weak areas. We need to shore up. We need Max and Hudson working tighter. And some of the talent stretched a little more. Michelle, Sirkka. We have a stay of execution, not a final verdict.'

'I wish I could respond more optimistically to what you're saying. But it's the worst possible situation given the people concerned. Michelle wants to move. Sirkka's heading for a breakdown – she's overstretched.'

Ansen's eyes locked hers and he put down the file of papers in his hands. 'There's something you should know about me, Wendy. I won't lose. I've done all the losing I intend to do in my life. I'm sorry for Hudson and Sirkka and the way this business is, but there are limits to sympathy. I intend to ride them hard. That's the only way there is.'

The chill of his voice made her shiver. She looked at him anew, half afraid of him because she only half understood him. She wanted to challenge this coldness, but the hot line phone on his desk interrupted. He hooked it, listened, put the phone down. He stood and swept together an armful of files. 'I'd better marshall weapons,' he said, 'they want me upstairs.'

'Upstairs?'

'The executive meeting. The "New Profile" agenda. This is it.'

'I wish I could be there.'

'So do I wish you could be there. I need all the help I can get. My luck has been out – ' The telephone went again and he took it and this time his voice became jaunty and laughing and he rang off with a beaming grin. 'Joey, my broker,' he said. 'Maybe it's an omen. My luck about to change.'

'Another personal coup?' she joked. 'Let me guess: now you're the majority voice in Harrods?'

He shrugged. 'Not quite. Yet. But a good personal purchase. Vellor and Marks, fine stock. Ever hear of it?' She said no, not particularly. 'It was a tip from a friend,' he said and then the veil of anticipation and boardroom-gearing came over his eyes and she knew it was time to go.

'Even better luck coming,' she pledged. 'Just you see.' But he hardly heard her. In trance-like concentration he took his case and exited.

In the boardroom the executive directors were settling in their plush red chairs as he arrived. Lee Wolf and Goldring were the last in – and then James Farrell made his customary grand entrance. Five minutes of round-about corporate talk ensued, but then the coffee came and the niceties were out of the way and the serious tactical play began.

'This month's agenda has been bashed around a bit,' James Farrell said, twitching his glasses towards Lee

Wolf. 'I believe it now revolves, like Kepler's universe, around a shiny star called the New Trading Profile?'

Wolf was immediately on his feet, issuing copies of a fat printed document, but Farrell was gratified to see that the American was stodgy of movement and already slightly sweating. 'I've issued a memorandum outlining the intention of this paper,' Wolf said, 'which you will all have received over the weekend – '

'And which makes no sense at all in view of the reviving figures,' Ansen put in directly.

Seven sets of hostile eyes turned on Ansen. James Farrell interjected, brusquely tripping through the report, 'It's old hat. It's a long-winded way of saying, let's go back to the sixties, to the way things were – '

Lee Wolf was outraged. He showed it, banging a fist on the tabletop. 'I'm suggesting a positive five-point plan to restructure the business. A new pyramid of control. A new division of Foreign Exchange, Equities and the Secondary Desk, with separate managers – '

'Which puts an end to Wendy,' Ansen said. 'Or does that mean, puts an end to me?'

Wolf rubbed his forehead with a bright American handkerchief. 'My point is that too much authority rests with too few people.'

'*You* want more?'

Wolf strove to remain cordial. 'I have my place. Corporate Finance is very satisfying. I'm not position-playing, Leonard. I'm trying to suggest a way of tightening the bank so that our overhead is controlled and our risk exposure diminishes – '

'You control the overhead by creating *new* managerial divisions?'

'Yes. I know it sounds like a paradox, but when one looks at the way the Capital Markets team – and let's face it, we're talking about *the core* team – operates, one can be in no doubt. And, since you've raised the issue of Wendy Foley I do think she is misplaced in this set-up. She has total discretion over who is hired and fired on the trading floor. She's flamboyant – '

'Wait a minute, Lee,' Ansen boomed, his voice getting tough. '*I* administer the trading floor and its policy. *I* chose Wendy Foley. *I* take responsibility for who works there and who doesn't. If there's a buck to pass, pass it here. And here it stops.'

Lee Wolf considered his options, sucked in air, and pulled the trigger. His eyes bent away from Ansen's as he started: 'The rot in Shane Longman is the administration of the trading floor. The risks are crazy and the risk evaluators are insane. People like Wendy Foley, Talbot, Max Lubin, some of those inexperienced kids.'

Leonard Ansen had had enough. He stood for a fight, threw the quarterlies across at Wolf. 'Go over them, Lee. Show us how bad it is – '

'It *is* bad – '

'The market is bad. But my people are turning it on its head. Yes, they take risks. Yes, they run on the edge. But what's this racket all about? It's the toughest odds outside Las Vegas, and you know it. I'll tell you what this "New Profile" is all about: it's about chipping away at the status quo.' He turned to address James Farrell. 'It's a ruse, James. Split the ranks, devolve responsibilities, separate working teams, smash the network.'

'But it has support, I perceive,' James Farrell said.

A rumble of disquiet ran round the table and Ralph Goldring raised a nervous hand. 'If I may coin one of Lee's phrases, that's the bottom line. Even before this paper is read and discussed, every one of us here has a sense of what is wrong – '

'The market is wrong,' Ansen persisted.

'And in the circumstances I think the resolution must be some kind of analysis and a vote.'

A silence fell and Farrell noted the nodding heads, and the glimmer of angry passion in Ansen's eyes. 'Let us not beat about the bush,' he said. 'All of us will have been aware of the difficulty of the last few weeks for Leonard's team. There were obstacles, but many of them have been overcome with comprehensive success. These figures are not shameful. In the circumstances I believe they are almost good. I think Leonard . . . and Wendy . . . must be proud of what they have achieved. But this – ' he stalled and spat the word; ' – *vote* is a trial-by-jury. A trial-by-jury of Leonard, and of his team . . .' As Farrell spoke he addressed everyone, but each time his gaze fell on Wolf a shrill inner voice goaded him: *it's not just Leonard; it's you. He wants your scalp more than anyone's. Ansen is right. This is just the beginning.*

When Farrell had finished, Lee Wolf seemed satisfied. 'I'm sorry it has to appear like this, James. But you have just defined the way democracy works. What is unfolding is fair and proper. I think Leonard must agree with that.'

'Analysis?' Ansen clucked.

'We all read and study this paper. We study the quarterlies. And then we define a limited period – I'd suggest a fortnight – in which your progress is considered and interpreted.'

The meeting broke up five minutes later, having skipped restlessly through some incidental concerns about the computer systems and the Settlements. Everyone seemed anxious to exit but Ansen and Farrell lingered. When they were alone Farrell said, 'I'm sorry, but the quorum has us.'

'It's a mistake to react to the market and blame the team, James.'

'It's style, Leonard. Some of your people are . . . noisy. The way they operate worries old fogeys like me.'

Leonard Ansen saw the tiredness in Farrell's face, the pallor, the fear. It would be cruel to debate with him. He rose to his feet. 'So we walk the line for another fortnight, eh?'

Farrell just nodded, but he spoke out as Ansen moved to leave. 'Want to do me a big favour, Leonard?'

'Of course.'

'Walk on eggshells. Keep the team moving.' He smiled for the first time. 'I know you'll make it.'

Ansen dialled Wendy and gave her a succinct account of the meeting, without elaboration or comment, and she rang off and locked the door of her office, shutting herself in. She found her Rubinstein tape and slipped it in the player, and then lit a candle and focussed on meditative peace. When she closed her eyes, usually, she saw seven steps to a tranquil cove. Now she saw the faces of Declan and Hudson and the risks she'd taken.

She stopped the music and opened her eyes. What the hell was she doing with her life? Thirty-four, a marriage in ruins, and hiding behind the world-worn façade of 'career girl'. She wasn't planning, she was *letting it happen*. Just like the marriage, a shambles of indifference dressed up to look like ambition. Had she ever *really* worked at it? Had she ever really worked to know Bruce? And the same inertia touched her career. Leonard Ansen was persuasive, sure. But wasn't that his great talent, the great ace-trader's talent? He led her magnificently, dangling carrots, promising an empire. His was the influence that brought aboard people like Hudson and Declan and Chas and Sirkka. His was the Grand Design. But what was in it for her? Where would it lead her, even if the long-shot maverick dream came true? More money, more ulcers? And if it failed . . . ? In a blinding moment Wendy had a vision of herself back at Citibank, in a saner and more sober job, with saner hours and saner crises and a far more manageable dream.

The phone rang and she was pleased to hear Howard Allen at the other end. 'You didn't call all week,' he said. 'I suppose you were absorbed in selling the house. You and Bruce – ?'

'Yes, he's making a settlement on me. I've already looked at an apartment I like.'

'Some lady,' he sighed. 'You know what you want.'

'Not always, Howard.'

'Terrific. Then maybe just once I can entice you – '

She groaned. 'I'm sorry, Howard. If you're suggesting an evening at the opera, I'm yours. Any longer-term arrangement – '

'Hey, hold on. You're embarrassing me. I hardly know you. And this is entirely professional. You've heard they call me a headhunter? Well, ever hear of Deutsch Premier? Mark Cantor?'

'A good bank.'

'They like what you've done with the Eurobond team at Shane Longman and they're restructuring in Europe.'

'Howard, I could have gone with Credit Lyonnais last summer – ' She heard herself begin a bald refusal and an alarm bell rang. 'I don't know, Howard. I'm tired, real tired. It's been a hard run and I must be getting old. It's started to take something out of me.'

'Just the point, dear girl. You're overtaxed at Shane,

and underpaid, I'd venture. Plus you have to ask yourself: are you happy to stay forever under Leonard Ansen's thumb and in his shadow?'

'What could Deutsch Premier offer me that's different?'

'Senior Vice President of Trading, that's what.'

She chewed her lip. 'Who do I have to talk to?'

'Mr Cantor himself. He wants to take you to lunch. Sooner, rather than later.'

Max had an idea.

It woke him at four, knifing through that staple thumbsucking dream that had him in Key West, or Mauritius, big game fishing with no ass in his pants. In the dream the sunshine sky darkened over and a hurricane came, and the hurricane gave him the idea. All week he had been tossing out lines, trying to turn up something novel. The fact that his brain was flat as a dead battery at this crucial time irritated him, and made him dive into doorways to avoid Wendy and Ansen. Ansen had even made the effort to take him to dinner, during which he outlined his fervent belief that Max and Max alone would hatch the serious recovery deals. But Max had failed – until now.

He showered and dressed in a race, and headed for town. He was stepping from the lift on Shane's trading floor at five when his single-minded progress was halted by the cry of a baby. *I'm hearing things*, he told himself but when he seated himself in his octagonal box the burping cry came again and a man's voice, distinctively American, said, 'Baba, baba, baba, *baba*.'

'Hudson!'

Hudson Talbot was shirtsleeved and casual, and

wearing a baby harness. A pen was fixed behind his ear and his hands were full of telex papers.

'This has got to be a joke! You *still* haven't fixed yourself up with a nanny?'

'No joke. It's like Declan said. Boredom called me back to the fray. I couldn't stand another night of it. The waiting – ' His voice faltered and he turned away to fuss with a squawk box marked 'Tokyo'.

Hannah, perennial Hannah, walked down the aisle with a silver tray bearing coffee mugs. 'Your terminals open again?' she said. 'Everything working?' Hudson nodded and she patted the baby's head. 'Now remember, when he sleeps bring him down to me. When he wants a feed, let him feed on demand. This is a crucial time in a child's life and you need to get it right.'

'Thanks, Hannah. You're a darlin'.'

Hannah took a pouch of screwdrivers from her belt and hurried away in search of faulty relays. 'She missed her calling,' Max said, unsure how to resume the talk with Hudson. 'Should have been a mechanic – or a nanny.'

'I'd settle for a nanny any day.' Hudson sat and swigged the coffee, which steeled him. 'I seem to be coping, Max. I'm surprising myself. Every day that goes by I feel stronger, and the reason I feel stronger is the kid. I don't have Alex . . .' his voice rippled, 'but I have Jamie. And in having him, I have, I guess, love.'

Max advanced cautiously: 'Did she call?'

'Alex?' He shook his head.

'Maybe it's a phase, something she has to exorcize from herself. Maybe a post-natal depression?'

'What I want to do now is focus on the problems of Leonard and Wendy. I know the flap. I know it's the killing time . . .' Hudson rambled on, confessional and intense, promising to turn the bonds market on its head.

'I have something better,' Max joined, glad to be back in the working groove. 'A flash of inspiration from on high, Hudson. Something that drove me from my bed.'

'Tell.'

'Give me an hour.' He slapped Hudson's shoulder. 'Feed that damn baby while I draw up a plan to conquer Planet Earth.'

An hour later Hudson, Hannah, Sirkka and Wendy – earlier than usual at their stations because of the crisis – were gathered at Max's dug-out, looking at his Reuters terminal which displayed what looked suspiciously like a weather chart. 'Commodity prices,' Max told his audience. 'The grain harvest is a major influence on the US economy. Now, what affects the grain harvest?'

Hudson ventured, 'Weather?'

'Specifically, the sun! So my target is simple. I need to anticipate the hours of sunshine the Mid West can expect over the next twelve weeks, thus indicating the size of the harvest and the consequential effect on food productivity figures – '

Wendy made a noise close to an exasperated grunt. 'Max, I know you specialize in the unobvious, but isn't this a bit extreme? It's the realms of science fiction.'

Max ignored her, faced Hannah. 'Can we use the microwave feed to get the US networks? I need the constant weather forecasts.'

'Who's paying for this insanity?'

Max shrugged. 'Special Projects Department?'

'I haven't heard about that one,' Wendy said.

Chas rushed up behind her, wide-eyeing Hudson. 'Do you know where Declan is?'

Max quickly squared the picture but Wendy was intent on progress: 'I need movement, Max, and simple bullseye logic.' She turned to Chas. 'Your desk?'

Chas was faultlessly fast. 'French franc is all over the place. Can't read it at all. Dropped three ticks. We can square the open yen position, no problem. Still short on Deutschmarks, long on the dollar.'

'Hear that?' Wendy asked Max. 'That's the English language. The way I like it to sound.'

'Suit yourself,' Max said. 'I can build a new programme here that will have the street wetting itself with excitement.'

Ansen arrived, crumpled from sleep but attracted by the bodies around Max's station. He listened to a quick recap of Max's lunacy, imagining as the story unfolded the kind of response that might come from upstairs. He laughed aloud when Max was finished.

'Do it,' he said. Max clapped his hands and goaded Hannah: 'Get me the CNN, whatever you can get. Fast as you can.'

The bewildered group disbanded but Wendy followed Ansen towards the lift. 'Can I talk to you, Leonard?'

His step didn't falter. 'Sure thing. I need to talk to Lloyd's, so I'm short on time. Talk as we go.'

'I don't think you're doing the right thing. With Max.'

He gave her a cruel side-glance. 'Don't tell me I have to fight *you* as well? Max's genius is his longshot instinct.'

'Agreed. But sometimes – maybe just sometimes – a little traditional caution is a good idea. We are under heavy fire. The spotlight shines right here. The accusation is risk-taking and squandering and maverick investment . . .'

'What's the matter, Wendy? A touch of the white feather? You never seemed a coward to me.'

The words, and the bald directness, hurt and deeply shocked her. He continued towards the lift and the look on his face – the faraway one-track self-interest – felt like a profound betrayal. 'Cowardice doesn't come into it – ' she began, but he talked over her:

'The one thing Lee Wolf won't do is make me hide in a cupboard. I do it my way or not at all.'

'James Farrell *asked* you – '

'To hell with James. Same goes for James as goes for Wolf. *My way*, Wendy. That's all that matters.'

She watched him closely for what seemed like a long time, and her thoughts were amok.

He said, 'Maybe you need a break, girl? A couple of days won't hurt anything.'

She felt like screaming in his face. 'All I'm saying is that Max is sometimes insane. And James Farrell is the force that keeps you – and me – here.'

They stopped side by side to wait for the lift and she thought swiftly about devotion, dedication, love; and their hair's-breadth relation to fear and hatred. 'We're a good team because we understand roles, Wendy. Yours is to make sure the bond room runs the way I want it to run.'

She stared hard at him for a full minute, confused by her turmoil, rethinking her trust. At last she said, 'You know, I think you're right about that break. And I think you're very generous to offer it, considering what you said about Sirkka and Michelle.'

His expression filled with fury and then the lift came and he stepped into it and kept his back to her as the doors sighed shut.

By late afternoon Max's familiarity with imbedded

cumulonimbi and nimbostrati had advanced considerably, and Hannah was hounding down a US cable link. He was feeling good, adrenalin high; so good and so high in fact that the call from Dover police locating his Bristol in Northern France just made him smile. It was a lesson learnt about whistlestop women, and about laundromats; chalk it up to experience.

At four thirty he crossed to the Spanish Steps wine bar for a tipple and a sandwich. Michelle Hauptmann was there, alone, sipping a Tavel. She looked sad. 'It's hell in there,' he said lightly and she gave a half-smile adding, 'It's hell everywhere.'

'They tell me you're spreading your wings?'

'I have till Saturday to decide.'

'I thought you were decided?' He stopped and peered. 'This is right out of line and you can just tell me to mind my own business but . . .' He saw her fluster already. 'Why do you always keep your head down? Literally and figuratively. You're a very lovely woman – and I'm *not* trying to charm my way into your diary – but you hide.'

'Maybe that's why I hide. I don't want to be just a very pretty woman.'

'More than that. You're a hot trader. I've seen them come and go in my time, but you have class. You have a cool head and that's the key. That's why it works for you. And yet you don't seem to want to do anything about it. Other people in your position, with your talent, would lobby and push and beg for an upper rung – '

'Maybe that's why I'm pitching for the States.'

'Credible, yes. But that's not the story. A little birdie told me you're going into Corporate Finance. That's a damn secretarial post – '

She looked at him with icy clear eyes. 'You know

what I hate about the British? They always want logic and answers. The Sherlock Holmes spirit, I expect.'

'My Sherlock Holmes spirit tells me Michelle Hauptmann keeps gypsying because she has something stuck in her like a thorn that stops her from having a good time.'

She hesitated, then gave a pearly smile that thawed her eyes. 'I like Shane Longman. I like you, Max.'

'I'm flattered. No, flattened. A compliment from Michelle!'

'Stop it,' she joked. 'I'm not mean with praise. Declan McConnochie tells me I keep his ego alive.'

Max saw her delight on speaking Declan's name. He nudged her. 'I'll let you in on a secret. I know the Shane staffers better than anyone. I know them all. I know their weaknesses and their strengths. And I observe that there's only one person on the floor with a mystery akin to Michelle Hauptmann. And that's Declan McConnochie. He's a great good fellow who's lost in the universe. Do you know what I mean?'

She became serious again. She thought a moment and said, 'I wish I could agree with you.'

'You don't believe his heart is in the right place?'

She was about to answer but the waiter called Jack ran up and told her she was wanted at her station. She stood, put back her rosé wine and slapped the folded newspaper she had been reading into Max's lap. 'My star sign says it's time to leave,' she said. 'I only obey them when they're that drastic. Try yours.'

She was gone and Max sat pleasantly in her perfume and opened the paper. He was feeling good – and then suddenly he was feeling bad. A corner headline caught his eye: *Lowenstein Nets Vellor and Marks.* He ran desperately through the column, his stomach turning. Abandoning his sandwich, he hurried back to Shane and called Ansen on the first phone to hand.

'Leonard, have you seen the stop press on Vellor and Marks?'

'You're going to tell me we scored?' Ansen came back happily.

'I take it you bought?'

'Just as you advised. A lot.'

'And you discussed it with Hal Lowenstein?'

A silence, then: 'What are you telling me, Max?'

'Lowenstein has been secretly negotiating a big buy-out. The prices will go through the roof. I just thought about your relationship with Hal. Dear chums, and all that. I just thought – '

'The insider trading cuss.' He let the obscenities roll. 'Just think what Lee Wolf could do with that.'

'I think you need legal advice, Leonard.'

SIX

Clay
Pigeons

Max's instincts were deadly, because forty-eight hours later the dreaded, ominous summons arrived: the DTI's lawyers wished to interview Leonard Ansen. In the intervening time Ansen had thought of calling Hal Lowenstein but, replaying events in his mind, he knew for sure it could be nothing more than appalling coincidence. Some circumspect phone calls to fellow traders filled in the picture: Lowenstein had been interested in an acquisition like Vellor and Marks, a digital software producer, for months. 'So it was common knowledge?' Ansen asked a pal hopefully but the voice at the other end chuckled, 'On the contrary, Leonard, it was the best kept trade secret in years.'

Cautioned, Ansen had consulted his lawyer James Fineman, who advised a cool head and crossed fingers. 'These things can slip by unnoticed,' Fineman lied reassuringly. 'So don't fret 'less you have to.'

But now Ansen had to.

An hour after receiving the recorded delivery missive Ansen was in Fineman's office at the foot of Fleet Street.

Fineman was an old friend, a fine friend from schooldays at Fettes, who possessed the instincts of an Indian scout and never wasted any time getting to the point. He studied the letter, clicked his intercom and called for whiskies – the traditional schooldays salute they never forsook – then laid it on the line. 'You've walked into a minefield, Leonard, there's no use beating about the bush.'

Ansen found himself blethering: 'James, I assure you there's no complicity here whatsoever. It's like I said: I asked my broker to position some capital for me, I'm always trying to move it to advantage, there's no big deal about that. He bought a chunk of stock and a week later Lowenstein's put in a cash bid for the company. Their interest in the company was totally unbeknownst to me–'

'But your friendship with Hal Lowenstein isn't exactly a state secret and the DTI naturally assumes prior knowledge.'

'That's nonsense, James. It's like I told you. I'm just repeating myself. I saw this coming – '

'You're avoiding Hal for the time being?'

'He's out of the country. But I'm not sure avoiding him is a good idea. I have nothing to hide. Neither has Hal. Ask him. Hal will swear an affidavit, I'm in no doubt of that.'

'Take it easy, Leonard.' The whisky had arrived and both men devoured it with unusual relish. 'Insider trading is the one blemish that's not erasable in the City. It's cancer, it's the death kiss. We both know this and we both know the fragility of your position at Shane. So far this is all just conjecture and dark hints. Now the DTI has moved in. But it's a test of nerve as to how we respond. We must be firm and surprised and derisive. This is patently absurd!' He took up the letter from the DTI's lawyer and flung it into the air. 'We are busy men, we have no time for this rubbish! If they have specific charges, let's have them. But they need substantial *evidence*. This is just the evidence of coincidence.'

Ansen laughed without humour. 'You think they'll back down so easily?'

'Let me talk to them.' Fineman tapped his forehead with a sage, earnest expression. 'I have a way with words. I call it my anti-litigation line. Wins every time, even with women.'

For the second time in two days they pored carefully over the background to the Vellor and Marks purchases and Fineman repeated his inferred summary till it was a sweet, agreed recitation. Then they split, with Fineman's assurance that he would confront the DTI's lawyers and come back to Ansen within the day, and Ansen took a cab to Soho where he'd agreed to lunch with James Farrell.

Farrell's choice of restaurant was Creole and Ansen looked with scepticism at the menu that Farrell insisted was health-oriented. 'I have to keep an eye on my innards,' Farrell said conspiratorially, ordering the goat's milk curry. He leaned forward and winked. 'Actually this place is the great secret I keep from myself. Otherwise my routines are religious; I never looked better.' His gaze flickered slightly as he demanded, 'Tell me I never looked better.'

'You never looked better.'

'While I was sitting here waiting I was trying to work out what it was about you that so endeared me. Now I know. It's simply that you're an agreeable fellow . . .'

Farrell talked on, long and windy and roundabout. The circles of conversation made Ansen dizzy and he knew Farrell had invited him for something other than a confrontation about DTI rumours. He breathed easy, but then he focussed up. Farrell had a message to deliver, and the message wasn't coming over. He interrupted a speech:

'I appreciate the compliments, James, but what exactly are you getting at?'

Farrell's face creased. 'Let me postulate a hypothesis. If the books don't come up to scratch . . . if the jury decides you're out – ?'

'We won't *be* out, James.'

'That's fine fighting talk, Leonard, but the board is heavily weighted. I'm on your side, but even if I started today I couldn't shift the support from Wolf's backers. The restructuring makes a kind of insane sense, even you can see that?'

'You're the top cat, James.'

'Chief executive is a cruel fallacy, Leonard, and you know what I'm saying.' He stooped forward in his habitual emphasis. '*Be prepared*, Leonard, that's all I'm saying.'

'You mean, scout a new position along the street?'

Farrell couldn't bring himself to acknowledge the comment. He sat back and made a ceremony of pouring Perrier and squeezing in a lime. 'The food's spiffing, isn't it? Encountered it for the first time in a little place amongst the strippers and hookers on the rue St Denis in Paris. Made me run off to Martinique. Piquant is the word, isn't it?'

At Langan's at precisely the same time Wendy Foley was concentrating with some difficulty on the velvet persuasion of Howard Allen, headhunter, and Mark Cantor of Deutsch Premier, a vibrant spark of a man with winner's eyes. She had, as she promised, taken time out from Shane and she had used this time to commence her home move, but the vagrant hours were pressing hard on her now, all the more so since a curious rumour about the DTI's interest in Leonard Ansen had drifted her way. Her head was full of anxiety to get back to the bank and back to Ansen but she shook herself and tried again to concentrate on what these men were saying.

She liked the look of Cantor from the moment they met. He had a young face, an ageless frame – and wore sneakers. Howard had told her to expect a hard-hitting pro of the European school, so she'd fixed in her mind a picture of austere earnestness; but his toothy grin, let alone his sneakers, smashed the preconception. He explained with charm: his company had a charity games day in progress and he had been delighted to partake; he'd just had time to shower and pull on some fresh Lacostes, and here he was. He hadn't wanted to miss this lunch on any account. He'd observed Wendy's career from afar and liked what he saw and read. Others referred glowingly to her; some at Citibank said she was a future City superstar. 'Superstar' was trade-speak of the eighties, a much over-used word. But he had a feeling about Wendy Foley, and his feelings rarely betrayed him.

'Not just that,' he winked. 'But I hear you are a very spiritual woman, a woman enchanted by all things Eastern, by Buddhist philosophy – ' Wendy shot a black look at Howard Allen. 'This profoundly impresses me, for I have long contended that to serve commerce, one must first serve heaven.' His eyes lifted fractionally towards the gilded roof.

Wendy smiled. 'I know someone quite like you. I've been sitting here trying to work out who you remind me of – ' she was thinking warmly of Peter Longman – 'and now I know, it makes it easier.'

'To say yes?'

'To understand you. This other man isn't the self-made success you are but he is a good man. It's comforting to see your informality. I don't know why but I sometimes think these attributes are linked. It's impossible to be totally one-track and keep a balanced control. One needs perspective and variety.'

'As you have.' Cantor took a slim manila file from his case and slid it in front of her. It bore the Deutsch Premier logo and, neatly stencilled, her name in all its glory: *Wendy Karen Foley*. 'This is a key management position in our restructuring. Here's the prospectus. Salary, bonuses that will make your mouth water, everything. Naturally we'll provide you with an apartment in Frankfurt. One of the best in a block we ourselves have developed – '

'In Frankfurt?'

'I said restructuring in Europe,' Howard put in. 'It includes unlimited travel expenses, of course.'

Cantor saw Wendy's fluster. 'You have, er, family commitments here in London?'

'N-no, none at all. I just – ' She started a sentence that led nowhere and felt herself blush. 'I'm very English, I suppose. When it boils down, a bit of a home-bird.'

'But you're ambitious?' She couldn't deny that. 'And you're bright enough to know that you have to move somewhere beyond Shane Longman. You have built up that room, you have *succeeded*. And, my information tells me, there is no room at the top in that institution.'

'I have been very, very happy there.'

'But perhaps this figure will ensure your greater

happiness.' He opened the prospectus and stabbed a forefinger at a blocked-out sum: *$200,000 plus bonuses as detailed below, and stock options.*

'It is attractive.' But her mind had gone woozy and unclear. Even the effort of thinking it out was painful. She could see herself working with Mark Cantor and laughing with Mark Cantor. She could see the door plaque that said *Wendy Foley, VP Trading.* She could see the dollars and the savings, but she could not see that flight to Frankfurt, or her everyday life there, or a moment of formal farewell to Leonard Ansen. Cantor was staring at her like an hypnotist. She drew herself up defiantly. 'I need time.'

'And I need a veep, Wendy. Now. I'm sorry, but I want a decision inside the day. Preferably at this table.' He slapped Howard's arm affectionately. 'Tell her, Howard. A man like me is overwhelmingly flattered by a spontaneous acceptance. It will colour my view of Miss Foley forever. Tell her.'

'I think you must go for it,' Howard Allen urged.

'My reply will disappoint you, but isn't it a woman's privilege to be fickle?' She sent her most alluring smile. 'I need time. That's the best decision you'll get from me today.'

'I'm sorry we have to end it like this,' Cantor said. 'I'd hoped to lure you back to the sports centre with me, for the rest of the games day.'

'Next time,' she smiled.

'But I'll have my next decision – ?'

'Within twenty-four hours.'

It was a sombre Leonard Ansen that greeted Wendy at the door of his office and instructed his secretary that they were not to be disturbed.

'I've heard a nasty snatch,' she started but he jumped ahead of her, diving for the deep end:

'It's true. And alarming that you're hearing a whisper.' He poured some liquor from his cabinet and offered it to her. 'The DTI lawyers want to talk to me. It's a nonsense of course, a confusion of coincidence about my purchase of stock and Hal Lowenstein's purchase of a company – '

'Who else knows?'

'My secretary, my lawyer, you. I lunched with James but I couldn't bring myself to tell him. Maybe I couldn't bring myself to face up . . .' He paced like a cat, quaffed his drink. 'I don't know, it's so absurd, so tragically bad-timed. When I got back I sat here and thought it over and of course I realized I'd better square up to it. I've sent a memo upstairs, but it isn't for circulation. I want them all to hear it at once.' He stalled, caught her eye. 'But I wanted you to know first.'

'But there's no reason why your personal circumstances should colour your ability to run the department. If anyone suggests – '

'Oh, Wendy, for heaven's sake, be realistic. Look at the ramifications. Quite apart from any insider scandal, look at my personal position here.'

'Don't insult my intelligence, Leonard. I *know*. But I also know your integrity. So does James. When it comes down to it so does Lee Wolf and all the others. There have been incidents in the past when we have lost contracts because you refused to sub-contract issue to an underwriter who stabbed someone somewhere in the back. You yourself fired two of our smartest kids because you knew they were bending towards insider tricks.'

'You underestimate the seriousness of Lee's intentions. No smoke without fire, Wendy. All that.'

'If you stoop to his game, you're lost.' She paused, held his eye. *'We're* lost. I recall you telling me about that stock purchase. I know you were dealing honestly. If I can go witness – '

But she had lost his attention. He was drifting, lost in a wooden gaze out of the window, imagining a wild and unhappy future.

'Is that it?' she said sadly.

For a long moment he didn't hear her, didn't answer. Then he stirred, filled his drink again and said, 'I just thought I should let you know the prognosis.' As she moved towards the door he mumbled to himself, 'It's a paradox. I've built this bank into one of the most aggressive in town and yet I can't invest my own money without walking into shit . . .'

Clear-headedly and without hesitation Wendy returned to her office, called James Farrell's secretary and asked for an urgent meeting. She was instructed to come up immediately and she did so, unthinking, fully on auto-pilot, blankly certain of all she must say.

Farrell was seated in the gloom of an unlit office on a dark day, scowling over a paper that might well be Ansen's memo. He didn't stir, didn't even recline in his chair when Wendy spat out her concerns about Ansen's possible trial-without-jury. In a grim, flat monotone he said, 'I don't want you involved any more that you must be, Wendy. There is a meeting being scheduled with Leonard right away. Depending on the availability of the board executives it's likely to happen tomorrow when, I believe, Leonard is expecting a clearer picture of his DTI position.' Farrell heard his own crusty bark and sucked air. He dragged up a smile. 'What I'm trying to say is, if worst happens I want to try to keep some of the people who built up this floor. I want to keep you – '

'Leonard Ansen built up this floor. Be in no doubt of that.'

Farrell raised his voice, his ire visible. 'I don't need you or anyone to tell me what Leonard contributed to the bank. I'm talking practicalities, Wendy. In a couple of days the team position comes up for final review. Leonard's the man responsible. He's the one who has to give account for himself, and for the team. First and foremost *he's* on trial. Nobody says the jury is unbiased. So Leonard's in the firing line, he's under glass, he's exposed. He has to be squeaky clean, word perfect, delivering. If he's not, he's gone. If I have to accept that, I will. And if that *is* the case, I've got to provide for myself and my future and the future of Shane. I've got to fight to keep what I need. And if I lose Leonard Ansen I may need you more than ever.'

The speech, despite its fury, moved Wendy. But still she said, 'I know how fickle business life is. I know how boardroom wars can be. But I also know and value truth. I *know* that the future of Shane Longman, in terms of growth and success, rests with Leonard.' She bent her gaze. 'I don't want you to perceive what I have to say as a threat. But I intend to stand beside Leonard as he stood beside me so many times. The bottom line, James, is that if Leonard goes, I go. And this isn't a retaliatory device. It would hurt me very much to leave you behind, and all the other friends on all the other floors.'

Declan tried. He did try. But it's a hard task to put a woman like Michelle out of your mind and shut and bolt the passion-proof door and throw the key away. Harder still when all your working life you've made an art of negotiating entries and vanquishing locks.

The busy days at Shane proved useful. With great concentration Declan filled his life with panic and rush. Schedules were excessively tight, deals were breaking, baby Jamie needed a constant brother. Declan dashed – even managed to go unshaven for a day – but the hint of Michelle, a problem and a promise, remained on the fringe of everything, every moment, every day.

As Saturday loomed, despite all distractions, he cracked. He was driving home with Hudson, his car again lost to the tow-truck, when the constant tide of Eurobonds, gilts and Treasury notes beached him. It was easy to see what was happening: Hudson was reorienting, immersing himself as needed in an over-flow of work-work-work. The baby lolled, asleep, in the crib pushed in the back seat but Hudson had forgotten his existence. They rounded corners too sharply, accel-erated unnecessarily. 'Go easy,' Declan cautioned but Hudson was keen only to listen to himself and his analysis of Max's weather vision. 'It could work,' Hudson was drawling. 'If Max can offer up projections that figure, someone might buy in big . . .' He jumped a fence to the next one: 'The Shapiro deal also interests me. He wants to know if we'll accept co-management on the Security Pacific stuff that came to Sirkka as a trade-off via the Bank of America – '

Hudson missed a red light at a roundabout and Declan cut in: 'What about the kid?'

'The kid?'

'A mother for Jamie. I know I'm being personal, but how long can you drag the child into the City like this? Maybe you should seriously start looking for Alex?'

It was raining and the evening had a murky sadness. In the dark of the car Declan could only see Hudson's silhouette against grey. The jaw clenched and chewed tensely. After a minute Hudson said, 'I just sense that she doesn't want to be found.'

'But when you *love* someone, Hudson! Surely love is a creation like the damn baby. It's something permanent.'

'People die, Declan. Love dies.'

'Through abuse, neglect or old age. Sure, I can almost believe that. But if it's there it doesn't just . . . go away. If you really love someone . . .' His thoughts flew inwards. If he loved Michelle he must support her in whatever she wanted to do. But love is a two-way street; two people are involved. Of course she wasn't *obliged* to return his love – that perfection of the two-way street was a certain outsider now – but it was right that he should labour to show his love, to offer her whatever security or amusement she might take from it. He should not hide, as he was lately doing, nor should he allow her to carry away the conviction that he was no better than an opportunistic rake who'd stumbled upon her – a kind and accessible girl – and tried his luck. The mere notion of this likelihood made Declan's pulse jump. Time had run out, he had to get to her . . .

'Tell me about your acquisition of the Pacific issue?' Hudson asked excitedly. 'I think if we can lure them to us on an exclusive-trading basis – '

'I have to bale out, Hudson. Drop me at a taxi rank, at the station. I promised Michelle,' he lied.

Hudson was paddling too fast to object. 'I want to open some inquiry lines tonight,' he mumbled and he veered off towards the station park.

In the cab bound for Michelle's Declan found himself rehearsing like a ham actor. He'd spoken to her three times in five days, once in an exchange that cost him no more than ten syllables. There was much ground to make up, and the misunderstandings of a year to be overcome. With this woman of all women, on this night of all nights, he must not, could not fail.

At reception in the hotel Andy tugged the frogging on his unnecessary tunic and looked uncomfortable. 'I, er, don't know if she's in,' he said. 'Maybe I should ring upstairs.'

'Come on, Andy, I'm not the bailiff.'

He stepped out of the lift with an optimistic spring in his step. Last time he had stood here he had been limp-kneed and doped with tiredness. Now he was fresh and full of love and ready to make her understand. Saturday was a day away but New York seemed very distant. He could smell her, he could feel her, he was home again.

He knocked, and the door was opened. He felt himself smile, and he felt the smile freeze, muscle by tiny twinging muscle. A man, a blond attractive man with a T-shirt that said *Surf Berliner*, frowned down at him.

'I . . . was . . . looking for . . . Michelle?'

The German surfer smiled some sunshine. 'I'm Bruno. She's not here but you can come in and wait . . .'

SEVEN

Who Wants To Be a Millionaire?

Friday broke bad for Ansen. At five he was awake, ceiling-gazing, reflecting on last night's meal with Wendy and luxuriating in his emotional ease. The call from James Fineman took away all this cheerful enthusiasm. 'I spoke to the people,' Fineman said with a catch in his voice that boded ill. 'I was surprised by their truculence.' He coughed. 'They're talking criminal proceedings.'

'For God's sake, James! On what grounds?'

'You have a goblin in there called Mr Hope. Not at all apt. He's single-handedly crusading to clean up the City. The word I have is, he's looking for scalps.'

'Go for affidavits. Get Lowenstein, get my broker. I don't want you to waste anymore time.'

'I'm sorry it's going this way, Leonard. But your case is solid, don't you worry.'

'I do worry, James. The more this circulates without

formal challenge, the more hopeless my position. Let them act or shut up. I want justice.'

The anger was wasted, but he had to let go. In the shower he read a litany of vile language, punched the faulty tap head till he finally smashed it, then severely cut himself shaving. He rang Wendy at five forty to tell her the news and relate confirmation of the executive meeting scheduled for today. James Farrell had softened to the point of suggesting a delay, if not cancellation of the executive meeting, but Ansen had wanted to confront gossip and rumour head-on and had insisted on today.

'It's a mistake, Leonard. We're coming up to review time anyway. As you said yourself, we need some big deals to carry it. No amount of defending the rear will win it for us.'

'Maybe.' But of course she was right. He was panicking because for the first time he felt it slipping away. The wheel turns all the time, and this was the bad luck turn, the downward curve. Too much was happening too quickly and suddenly a full recovery seemed a miraculous unlikelihood.

Wendy divined his distress and took control. 'I'll put out one of my Maydays. We'll have a dealers' meet at eight thirty. We'll shake out whatever we can and try to pull out a rabbit by close of business . . .'

Both of them rang off in a welter of action that dispelled gloom. Here was a time for energetic imagination, for longshots, for calling in favours. Wendy rummaged for ancient notebooks and business cards, old friends, passing contacts, any slim chance. The phone jangled again. She snapped it up. 'Yes?'

'Sweetie, it's Howard.'

'Not at this hour, Howard.'

He hummed, offended. 'I thought we were better friends than that, Wendy. Any hour is fine for me?'

'It's just, I've got a little emergency.'

'I thought it might be a good idea to have a note on Mark Cantor's desk at nine. He's a good man who is impressed by that kind of professionalism. I think it's good to start well.'

'I'm sorry, Howard.'

All of a sudden his voice hardened. 'Listen, kid, I'm doing you one major favour here, in case you didn't notice. Chaps like Cantor don't grow on trees. I did a hard sell on you.'

'I didn't *ask* for a hard sell, Howard.'

'But you need it, Wendy. You need to open up your eyes. I heard about Leonard Ansen and a certain lucky purchase. It's not a pretty picture for Shane, or for you. Especially for you, dearest.'

'Don't patronize. I can look after myself.' She started to slam down the phone, but held it. 'Oh, and Howard? I'd be careful of what you're hearing and how you repeat it. Slander's a criminal offence – '

'Wait a minute, Wendy, don't go.' His tone rushed, and hushed. He gave a false fair-weathery laugh. 'I adore you, you know that. I am concerned for your wellbeing and that's all. You're moving into this new apartment tomorrow? Let me come over and help with the move – '

She cut in firmly: 'I don't adore you, Howard. I like you. If I made a mistake in leading you on, I'm sorry. We are friends. I appreciate your friendship. But I draw lines.'

There was silence down the line and then a harsh snatch of air. 'Do you want the Deutsch Premier job, Wendy? It's a quarter of a million dollars a year. Every woman in Europe would kill for it.'

She wanted to say the word 'No' but she couldn't make her mouth work. She thought of Ansen and she felt the guilt of disloyalty, but she knew she must be sensible. 'I need more time.'

'There is no more time. Cantor called me at midnight. He wants his answer now.'

'Well, he'll just have to wait. Goodbye, Howard.'

When she put the phone down her body was zinging, her head light. Was she crazy to do what she'd just done? A quarter of a million and one of the healthiest banks in Europe? She was tempted to grab the phone, call back, beg. Instead she took some deep breaths, lit a candle for focus, took her Shane book and dialled the Mayday.

By eight forty everyone had been briefed with a qualified candour and the dealing floor plunged into a mild but purposeful hysteria. Before the meeting Wendy advised Ansen to keep quiet about the Lowenstein scandal, and he agreed. There was no point in fuelling negative speculation. She told him about Howard Allen's remark – without detailing the Deutsch Premier deadliner – and he just shrugged. 'It's inevitable,' he said. 'But I have to ride it out and hope it doesn't spread too far before Fineman gets my case in order and knocks out the DTI. If I had the bank behind me it would be a lot easier and faster – '

'But you don't. And while James Farrell is doubtful you are seriously out-numbered for supporters – '

'Speak of the devil!'

Wendy swivelled to see James Farrell gliding brightly towards them. He stopped to stand on tiptoe and look over the trading maze. Sirkka came up with an appropriate expression of welcome and Jimmy Destry was fifteen paces behind. Farrell waved them away: 'You have Trojan tasks today, if I'm not mistaken. Go to them and don't waste time with welcoming parties.' He looked at Ansen. 'What's the word?'

'The DTI is talking criminal proceedings. A possibility, that's all. When they see my evidence – '

Farrell cringed. Very slowly he shook his head, eyes closed. 'I'll have to take this upstairs, you know that?'

'I appreciate your support, thank you.'

'Find the deal, Leonard. Just find it.'

Across the floor, in untypical early-morning relaxation, Max was chewing muesli and watching the Dodgers on CNN. Hudson Talbot, eyeing the tension between Ansen and Farrell from a distance, nudged up. 'Due respects, Max. I like the Dodgers more than most. But in the circumstances – ?' He dropped a key. 'Wendy's heading this way – watch it.'

'How's the baby, Hudson?'

'Fine health, Max. Which isn't on the cards for you, fella. Here she is.'

Wendy glanced at the glorious spectacle of the baseball and just grinned wearily. 'Anyone winning, Max?'

'Yep. Us. Take a pew.' He swung his chair round to take a call: Lee Ann Sorensen from Brennan's, a hotshot broker from the upper league. Lee Ann Sorensen bypassed chit-chat and asked for information. She'd heard of the weather tie-up and might want to buy into it. Max held forth.

'All right I'm impressed,' Lee Ann Sorensen said. 'I should keep away from the prairies this weekend.'

Max promised to fax her over his sales pitch: *Rainfall Trends and Grain Productivity in the US Farm Belt*. 'If we can forecast harvests we can forecast movements on the commodity index. Thus we can forecast interest rate movements and the direction of US bonds.' He leaned under his desk, pressed a button and ejected a video-tape from a standard VCR. He'd send that as well. 'Check it over. The video shows you how the weather scan looked. The report tells you what happened as a consequence of that weather. It fits.'

'Are we trading or fortune-telling?'

'Isn't it the same business?'

'You know of course about the Research Package we're developing at Brennan's?'

'I assumed that's why you called,' Max glowed.

'Many of our clients enjoy statistics . . . All right, I think we can buy it. If the price and royalty is right.'

'It don't come cheap.'

'I didn't expect it would. I'll hand it to Wendy Foley. Some of her wide boys occasionally deliver. I'll have Mr Ricardo call you after lunch with the deal.'

Wendy stood, head bowed, in front of Max. It was just one modest deal of course, but a genius display of the type they needed.

'Say nothing,' Max offered. 'Just give me a hug.'

She hugged him and felt ridiculously inadequate and childish. She shook herself and met his eye. 'Am I not accused of fostering flamboyance in the first place?' she demanded.

He laughed. 'I am your creation first!'

'Do you want to be the one to tell Leonard?'

'You do it.' He chucked her cheek. 'As penance.'

There was warm satisfaction in Wendy's voice as she dialled Ansen's extension on her hot line. 'Max delivered. I should be sent to trial. It's an impressive tie-up with Brennan's.'

'Not enough.' Ansen's tone was flat and defeated.

'What's wrong?'

'James just phoned down. The criminal slur sure

works. The executive meeting has been pulled forward. James says the feeling is they're out for blood.'

'I want to be there.'

'There's no point. James is right. Save yourself if you can. He needs you.' He sighed resignation. 'Good old Max. He might not have saved my skin, but he'll probably save everyone else's.'

The phone was dead in her hand and she was trembling with fury. She had to pace, to walk, to get out off the floor and into the street, to get air, to escape. She grabbed her coat off the rack and swept towards the exit.

Coming down the main entrance steps Wendy was confronted by the side-stepping ghost of Declan. He alone had been uncontactable for the Mayday routine, but that had not greatly surprised her. He opened his mouth to speak but she swerved past him, wrapped in the haze of her confusion.

She was out on the pavement, cannoning towards the Spanish Steps, when a flash of inspiration turned her on her heel.

Declan's hangover – a rarity that spoke for the depths of his upset – hung over. The throb behind his eyes necessitated shades, his hands shook, all his body was clenched in a clammy flu-like grip. The electronic hum of the lift, the murderous whisper of the Ventaxia corridor fans – everything conspired in a baton charge against his throbbing brain.

Where did last night begin and end? He remembered clearly the first surge of depression, and the sense of sudden aimlessness, but then he had rallied and come briefly back to his devil-may-care, fun-seeking self. There was that lovely girl in the Saab, whose eyes looked electric in the rearview mirror. He'd seen her suddenly as a potential saviour and acted on impulse. They were ships in the night, cars on the high street, but he had to catch her. So he did the only thing he could do: he reversed, foot to the boards; Audi meets Saab. She raged, of course, but he talked her round. They dined – or did they? – and she told him she was not the City analyst he had guessed at, rather she was a pilot who flew daily to Paris. She was romantic – or was she? – but at any rate they made a future date. After that his mood was high so he made it to String-fellows, alone, and then the night went crazy.

Sirkka was the first to find him on the trading floor. She embraced him in that big-sisterly way of hers. 'Did you hear about Max's deal? Into the Brennan's Research Package! It's the sort of radical team genius we needed to show. You missed it this morning. Wendy and Leonard clued us in on what's happening upstairs . . .' Her voice stuck as she narrowed her eyes on him. 'Good God, Declan!'

'I'm fine. Flu, that's all.'

'Flu? As in flew? As in flying? Yes, I can imagine you were sky high last night. What was the cause of celebration this time? A new girl in town?'

Michelle appeared just then, stepping from the lift that took her from Settlements. With a twinge of sheer agony Declan jerked his head away from her, but she saw him and came over. Sirkka saw the look on Michelle's pale face, saw Declan's tension, and decided to withdraw. 'I'll see you later, Declan. I had dinner last night with Aristotle from Berger's. You know him; I just wanted you to square me on how solid he is. He's circled half the Italy Deutschmark deal I'm building with Harry in New York.'

'He's OK,' Declan said without enthusiasm.

Sirkka mumbled a thanks and fled. Michelle stood in front of Declan's gaze. 'I'm sorry I missed you last night. Why didn't you stay? Bruno said – '

'Your fiancé.'

She felt indignant but held herself. 'Bruno is not my fiancé. Bruno is someone I have known for a very long time. His family and mine are very close. It's always been accepted that – '

'Oh. Arranged marriage? I thought they kept that in the Arab states, or India?' The scorn in his voice was heavy and savage.

'I don't have to give an account of myself to you, Declan – '

'Well why bother even talking to me? By all the signs I've a busy day ahead – '

He moved to walk away but she held his sleeve. 'What did you do to yourself? You look like wax warmed up.'

'I'm a free-booting bachelor; didn't you hear? I have no commitments, no responsibilities, no ties. I waltz round town drinking and seducing women – ' While he spoke he was trying not to hear the truth of those words; he was challenging her sympathy, hoping. He might find an answer in her eyes, but he could not bring himself to meet them.

'I want you to have dinner with us this evening.'

'Bruno, me and you? Cozy.'

'He doesn't want me to go to New York – '

Declan spoke before he thought: 'Will you? Go to the States, I mean?'

She lowered her head and he looked at her, at the soft rounds of her shoulders, the rage of her hair, all the rough-hewn grace of her. It took his breath away, like it always did. 'Bruno's father is a partner in a small investment bank in Munich. It's where I started.

They're very proud of their growth, and they deserve to be. Bruno is very proud of me. He calls me his hound dog. I'm out in the marketplace learning from the best – '

'So you learn the hoops and then you go home?' Declan tried to control the irritation in his voice, but it rang like a cathedral bell. 'Clever arrangement. I always said it: you have to hand it to the Germans for organization.'

He knew she was about to walk away but he dashed to beat her to it. 'Excuse me,' he said. 'I was rude to Sirkka, I feel I should speak to her.' Before she could respond he was halfway across the trading floor, feeling her eyes like red hot spikes in his back.

Sirkka switched off her babbling squawk box and greeted him gratefully. 'This is our do-or-die weekend,' she said, 'and it's starting to look like a team victory sweep. Jimmy and Chas are onto a good number. Max hit gold. And take a look at my Italy Deutschmarks.' She keyed up Reuters and handed a page of script outline to Declan. 'Everything's rosy – apart from the fact that some people are saying some funny things about Leonard Ansen's future.'

He wasn't listening. His eyes fixed on the Deutschmarks paper but burned through the page.

'Will she take New York?' Sirkka said gently.

'How the hell do I know?' Declan replied, flinging the page aside. 'For all I care she can try the Mongolia office.'

'Where are you going?'

'I left my favourite tie in a restaurant somewhere. Tell Wendy. I probably won't be back today.'

Lee Wolf's step was light with triumph.

He entered the boardroom last, his shirtsleeved casualness sharply contrasting with the conservative and funereal grey round the table. When he sat down opposite Ansen he smiled and Ansen dug deep to find a smile to match him. James Farrell had made no show entrance. Which was ominous. Ansen avoided Farrell's eyes: to his thinking, Farrell had already quit.

There was no minutes secretary, no preamble. Farrell opened in a jaded, almost careless voice: 'First of all I think it's right that we express our regrets that we find ourselves in this difficult position. It's especially lament-able since Leonard's team has progressed dynamically over the week – '

Lee Wolf's interruption was harsh and immediate. 'James, Leonard, I think we can dispense with polite speech-making. We gather that the DTI intend to insti-tute criminal proceedings against our Director of Bank-ing Activities. This is a catastrophe that washes out anything we've previously discussed – '

'I'm glad you phrase it like that,' Ansen cut in. 'Because it's important to specify that this concerns me, solo, and not the team. The team has exonerated itself – if that's the word – from any charges of inadequacy. Max's deal is representative of the kind of energy and talent that has made us big, and will make us bigger.'

The 'us' bothered Wolf, Goldring and a few shifting bodies.

'You may be right,' Goldring said nervously, all the time eyeing Wolf for approval. 'The team may not be at fault here. But the management of that team is seri-ously in question. If we have a criminal case against that manager – ?'

'Just a moment,' Ansen exploded. 'You – and the DTI – are moving on *an assumption* that I knew about the Lowenstein deal. My lawyers will prove otherwise.'

'But that's not how things are perceived on the street, Leonard.' Wolf twinkled, relishing every twist of the screw. 'Once people start to talk – '

'You sue them for slander and libel and whatever else it takes. Gentlemen, I'll say it in English. I have no charge to answer. Once Lowenstein and my broker and everyone else is called in to play, that will be clearly seen.'

James Farrell nibbled the edge of his spectacles, filled a glass of water, brooded. 'Perhaps, Leonard, if you offered to sell back the stock at purchase price?'

'Why should I do that? And admit complicity?'

Farrell stood and backed away and the beasts of the table stirred. Saltzman, a sewer rat, was whispering passionately to Wolf. Wolf leant forward. 'I think, Leonard, that you must do the honourable thing in the circumstances. We would like your resignation.'

'Anyone else?' Ansen swung his eyes round the table. Cross-questioning wasn't required. It was a close business but it was obvious that the majority vote was against him. The faces that supported him returned his gaze with bold sympathy, the others looked away. 'I expected some demonstration of allegiance, but this is the City, isn't it?'

'I'm terribly sorry,' James Farrell said very quietly.

Ansen sighed deeply and started the speech he had truly believed he would never make: 'I am comforted by the assumption that my team will remain structured somewhat as it is, and progressing in the way it is progressing. The improvement figures show you all how right that team is, how right that structure is. I would respectfully suggest that the new business plan be postponed indefinitely, or until such time as it becomes relevant to consider such a proposal. In the meantime I wish to commend Wendy Foley – '

'Do you agree to offer your resignation?' Ralph Goldring persisted.

It was as if the whole room held its breath. Ansen saw Farrell only, and Farrell's eyes were wet and tragic. 'The way it stands – ' Ansen began, and then suddenly the door burst open and Mabel, Wolf's secretary, made a sloppy, red-faced effort to introduce Peter Longman. The boardroom heard Longman before it saw him. Ansen grinned wide as Longman, out of sight, entreated a reluctant Wendy: 'Godammit, I didn't rush halfway across the country to do this by myself! Come on, it's not the Old Bailey in here!' A muttered exchange followed and Ansen thought of Wendy's guile, and stifled a laugh. Peter Longman entered, wind-bashed and alone.

Lee Wolf hurried to his feet, addressing Farrell. 'James, this is not the time – '

'You tell him,' Farrell answered pat.

Longman strode across the room, nodded to Farrell, threw a glance round the other members, then latched eyes on Lee Wolf. He hooked a chair and placed himself dominantly near the table top.

'When did you get into town?' Goldring asked pleasantly.

'An hour ago. And yesterday, and the day before, and the day before that. I feel like I've got a string of rubber stuck to my bum. I jet round the world defying laws of science. I am in two places at once.' He gave an evil smile. 'Sometimes wisely.' His eyes found Wolf again. 'Probably thought you'd seen the last of me, Lee? The proverbial sleeping partner.'

Wolf looked uncomfortable in his shortsleeved American shirt. 'Always good to see you, Peter, you know that.'

'That's reassuring.'

'Though sometimes – ' Wolf gave a buddy-happy shrug, 'sometimes you hit us at the wrong time.'

'Like now?'

'Fact is, you've arrived in the middle of a serious crisis – '

'Are there non-serious crises?' Longman was not grinning. He kept staring at Wolf. 'I was not made aware of the extent of your plan to redesign Shane Longman, Lee.'

Wolf threw up his hands. 'The document was mailed to you. I . . . we have nothing to hide.'

'You want Leonard Ansen out badly.'

'That's not the way it is, Peter. We have a particularly thorny problem – '

Longman drifted towards Ansen, then back. 'I shan't play cat and mouse. I listen to jungle drums. The *right* jungle drums. And I hear that Leonard has a spot of bother with the DTI.'

'Spot of bother! The allegation will be insider trading.'

'*Will be! Allegation*! Hold your horses here, Lee. This is the realm of maybe-maybe. No businessman worth his hundred grand talks this talk. This is kids' stuff. We speculate when we *have to* – that's what investment banking is all about – not when we feel like a fling.'

Lee Wolf rubbed a hand over his forehead. His supporters moved their feet round the table, scratched on their notepads. 'We've discussed this responsibly,' he resumed. 'Our feeling is that we must ask Leonard to go.'

'How gracious of you to consult me for an opinion!'

'You can be difficult to locate, Peter.'

'Rubbish!' Longman stood and pounded the tabletop. He addressed James Farrell directly. 'I'm not going to sit back and have this bank, or anyone in it, pushed around by some suit at the DTI. I've seen these fly-by-nights off before, I'll see them off again. We've all got to band together and stand behind our Activities Director and state the *true* position. Because truth matters.' He pointed at Wolf. 'This is *not* the time to grind personal or professional axes. Shane Longman is in fundamentally good shape. The market is down – so what else is new? But we are moving, and I intend to keep us moving, and Leonard Ansen is the motor that keeps us moving.'

Enraged, Wolf stood to match Longman's height. 'Gestures of solidarity are a waste, Peter. If there is dirt flying – '

'It seems to me, Lee, the dirt starts here in this boardroom. And I'll tell you something else: I didn't walk out on a critical bloodstock deal to opt for heartburn in a taxi doing seventy through central London – '

'No one asked you – '

'Yes, someone did ask me, you little shit!' Faces froze round the table. 'Someone who cares very much about this bank and where its direction lies. Wendy Foley asked me. She asked me to step into this fouled-up excuse for a boardroom and talk some sense. So now I'll talk sense and I'll talk it in the language most of you seem to understand. I *own* thirty per cent of this operation. My name is on it. Just because I don't participate in the everyday running of it doesn't reduce the value of my opinion. Or my ability to read a situation and respond.' He paused long and airily, examining every expression, drilling up the emphasis in his words: 'I have declined offers for my stock in this bank, offers that could have made me richer than even I know. I could have been a bloody millionaire ten or twenty times over – who the hell cares! I stuck with it because my old man was in here and my old man believed and my old man passed the dream to you, James – ' He slammed an accusing finger this time towards Farrell; Farrell went ashen. 'I stuck with it because I admired the values upheld by James Farrell and the values he passed on to you people, the executive members. My father wanted success. He wanted growth. But he also wanted integrity and a family sense of commitment, of cherished loyalty. I stand by that.'

Recovered from the bare-faced insult, Wolf kicked carelessly back: 'This is a bloody waste of time, if I may borrow the native expression.'

'Waste of time, Lee?' Longman left the tabletop and walked to Wolf's chair. He clapped the American's shoulder. 'Well, what about this for a waste of time? I'll tell you what I'm about to do. I'm going to leave here this minute and head for the Connaught. There I'm going to dine well and get a good night's sleep. And in the morning, if you haven't figured a way round this mess, I'm putting my stock on the market. I may be wrong, but I somehow suspect that your new partners won't be quite as congenial and easygoing as I.'

The movement of feet round the table became fast and frantic: pens scribbled on pads, an urgent whisper rose up. Lee Wolf's eyes were cold, dead fisheyes. Goldring moved to say something in his ear, but he elbowed him away. Peter Longman circled towards Ansen and punched an affectionate blow into his arm. 'Let's dine together tonight,' Longman said. 'I'm sure you need to hoist your spirits with all this crap circulating.' He moved on towards the door, then hesitated and turned back towards the table. 'Gentlemen, I ask you to review the sharp attributes of some of our people. Wendy Foley was prompt and impressive in overcoming obstacles to get this important story to me. I am honoured that she is on our side. I think you should share that sense of honour with me.'

As Longman departed and the meeting solemnly broke up Ansen fled as quickly as he could, his pulse racing, eager to be out, to wallow in his victory.

In the hall near the lift Wendy was busy by the alcove water machine, ostensibly pumping a polystyrene cup. She faked a look of innocent surprise and he just grinned at her, and hooked her arm, and guided her into the lift. It amused her to see his pallor – the shy white face of a schoolboy returning from the principal's office – but she said nothing.

'I can't think of any appropriate words,' he said.

'Don't be silly. You'd have done it for me.'

'If I'd thought like a vixen. I'm not as bright as you.'

They laughed as they reached the corridor that gave onto the trading floor. Max stood ahead of them, in animated conversation with Sirkka and Chas. All three turned apprehensively to greet them. The burning question was inescapable.

'We had some trouble upstairs,' Wendy said, 'but I think it's under control. Fully under control.'

Max's face split like a cracked egg. Sirkka gave a coo of victory and Chas whistled low. 'This calls for a party,' Max said. 'Does anyone know that Hudson is a French-class cook?'

Wendy moved on towards her office and Ansen caught her up. 'Dine with me?' he said.

'You have an engagement tonight, remember?'

'All right, have a drink with me now? We'll go across the street.'

She shook her head. 'Rain check. Right now I've got a call to make. To confirm a decision I made about an offer.' She walked off singing, somewhat wryly 'Who Wants To Be a Millionaire?'

EIGHT

The Gal That Got Away

The question was, of course, would Michelle take New York? Declan avoided it by lunching long and late at the Intercontinental in Hamilton Place and filling the middle afternoon with a string of long-promised calls to trader associates. By late afternoon he was fully himself again and the leaden guilt of deserting Wendy came down on him. He took the wheel of the Audi, nosed up towards Bayswater and slipped into automatic pilot.

It was time to get to grips with this Michelle-mania, to review his current situation and file her away appropriately. All right, he wanted her. In itself this unputdownable urge was interesting, but it was doubly interesting because he knew it was symptomatic of a wider phenomenon: he wanted a change of lifestyle. The old Declan was worn-out, spent as last year's firecrackers. The new Declan was . . . ? He stalled. Who was the new Declan? How versatile was his character? How deep? With what potential? He gave a little shudder. Was this the essence of Michelle's attraction? That the reflection he saw in her eyes – occasionally – was the spirit of hope for him? Michelle saw *something* good in him. She must do. Otherwise why would she bother over so many months? Why those languorous winter nights, the confidences, the sharing? She was his best friend. His only friend . . . He steered away from maudlin thoughts. He must not depend on her to rescue him. He must accept the responsibilities of manhood and do it himself. And surely *that* was the key to winning her – eventually, some day, some way: he must renew himself, act sensibly, grow up.

Without conscious decision the Audi homed sweetly in on Shane Longman and delivered Declan to its portals. He pushed through the swing door for the second time that day with a clear head and a confident heartbeat, bound first for Wendy's office and a sincere apology. Hudson Talbot met him coming from the lift and gave a pithy account of the afternoon's adventures. For the first time in days the merest flicker of a true smile lit Hudson's face. 'It's unofficial, but the Big Threat is out. Leonard Ansen is safe, the team is safe, we're home.'

'Safe is a delicate word, Hudson.'

The chubby American ignored the remark. 'Max is arranging a party for Sunday at his place. I'll do some cooking. Thanksgiving cooking, especially for the occasion. You make sure you come along. Bring a date. Bring – '

Hudson saw a sadness in Declan and checked himself. 'Bring a party hat, OK?'

'Is Wendy upstairs?'

'She's gone. Busy as a bee, full of victory. I'm delighted for her and for Leonard.'

'Is there anyone left up there?'

Hudson tapped his watch. 'Friday. End of a major battle. There's just a bit of mopping up going on'

'Michelle?'

Hudson shook his head. 'Sirkka finalizing her big deal. Maybe Leonard himself.'

'You didn't hear whether Michelle . . . ?' His heart sank with the question; he didn't want the inevitable answer.

'Ask Wendy,' Hudson hedged.

On the trading floor the lights were going down in the stations and the cleaners were shaking out their Hoover cables. It was wind-down time, and the glow of a special weekend was in the air. Sirkka alone was hooked industriously over her desk. She cast a humourless side glance as Declan drew up. 'Don't interrupt me, Declan. I've earned myself a special weekend. I have the deal with Ari locked, I'm home and dry.'

'I just wanted to apologize for my behaviour earlier. I mean, Michelle and all that.'

'I understand it must be difficult for you.'

He frowned down at her. Was that ironic bitchery he was hearing? Or her sympathy?

'Did Michelle speak to you about . . . going?'

'Uh-huh. She seemed confused and upset. I got the impression she really wanted to – ' she aimed an accusing look at him; ' – to go.' The American squawk box trundled over her last words. The voice of Harry Lemon, one of New York's poker-hottest Shane dealers, came over, tangled in the rage of a trading room in full flight:

'Sirkka? Presumably you've firmed up Ted Ulricht and Bucklehaus at Manufacturer's Trust?'

'Yes I have, as of fifteen minutes ago.'

'Genius! Good lady. When you're in town again we'll have a big dinner at the 21, right?'

'Suits me.'

'Tomorrow would be perfect.'

'Sorry to disappoint you. Tomorrow I'll be in the arms of a wonderful trader called Sven in distant Copenhagen.'

'There are no wonderful traders called Sven.' Harry Lemon coughed. 'You got to get yourself in order, girl. You're spreading yourself too thin. Get over here, permanent. That's my advice. That's what I told Leonard.'

'He needs me here.'

'Huh? You mean, he needs support in all these ragin' storms we've been hearing about?'

'The storms are abating, Harry. He's doing what you people call AOK now.'

'UK figures haven't been wunnerful – that's no secret.'

'But with deals like this little number we're all smiles over here. You should come and visit, Harry.'

At that moment Leonard Ansen pushed through the door and angled over. *I'm for it*, Declan thought, tensing; Leonard doesn't show his face round here unless it's a major drama. But Ansen just slapped his shoulder and frowned at Sirkka. 'No problems with your systems?' Sirkka shook her head. 'It's just I'm hearing some spooky stories of access codes being broken. Industrial espionage lives, it seems!' He smiled back to Declan. 'I presume you're here to admire Sirkka's ingenuity?'

'It's a nice deal.' Declan stepped aside with Ansen as the squawk box called Sirkka back to the specifics of the Deutschmarks deal that London and New York were sharing. 'Congratulations on the way everything worked out,' Declan said. 'Am I allowed to say that?'

Ansen grinned a non-boss grin. 'Yes, you're allowed to say it. But quietly. I'm flattered that everyone's so . . . enthused. Though I thought it best to respectfully side-step Sunday's party. I appreciate Max's and Hudson's sentiment, but I somehow felt my participation identified, shall we say, battle lines.'

'I know what you mean.'

'But you'll be there, I hope?' Declan nodded, extended a hand to Ansen. 'Well, I'll say congratulations again. I'll be in there slugging with you come Monday.'

'You'd better be. I want some happy surprises from you, my boy. I want rewards.'

Declan mumbled a goodbye to Sirkka and dragged his heels down the corridor.

'Surprises from Declan?' Sirkka joked to Ansen. 'Isn't that like looking for oil from Arabs?'

Ansen was staring hard after Declan. 'I don't know. I think he's got plenty up his sleeve. Does any of us know the *real* Declan? He's still the only City man I've met who can quote Shakespeare to me while totting up his winners from the back of the *Sun*.'

They laughed – and then a junior five stations away popped up his head to summon Sirkka. 'Call for you,' he shouted.

'Aristotle, on line fifty-three.'

'Friend Ari,' Ansen said with warmth.

Sirkka took the line with a breezy show. Ansen heard her say, 'Make it quick, Ari. I've a plane to catch to Copenhagen in about two hours. I'm planning a royal weekend . . .' The gaiety died in the next breath. 'Say that again, Ari?' And then: 'You've got to be bloody joking, mister!' Ansen *saw* trouble. Sirkka's eyes became fierce wet slits. Her knuckles froze. Her posture became ramrod straight.

She flung the phone down, missing the cradle by a yard. She kicked off her high-heeled shoes, fisted the terminal top, tossed the Deutschmarks file into orbit.

'The bastard! The filthy, double-dealing bastard, Aristotle. He's dropped me in it. He's pulling out of the deal.'

The deal was too big, the day was too significant. Ansen could not restrain himself. 'It can't happen, Sirkka. He *must* take it.'

Her hands were violently shaking. 'He won't. He's simply out.' She fought for control. 'Do we have any recourse?'

'He didn't *buy* them?'

She stammered. 'Well, I trusted him. I had no reason not to. Everyone told me . . . Declan's dealt with Berger's many times. He said they were fine – '

Ansen's voice raised. 'Berger's might be fine, but *Ari* is the one you're facing up here – '

'I checked him out, for God's sake. He has taken bigger positions!'

'I'm sorry, Sirkka, but you cannot lose this one. Not after all we've been through, and with the final vote still not confirmed. I insist you hold it together.'

'But how can I?'

'You'll have to get in here midnight on Sunday and hit the Far East market as soon as it opens. Maybe call Lewis, see if he's got any institutional clients over the weekend. Shuffle the deck, but find a card.'

He walked away, briskly, running from his anger. Sirkka was nauseous, feeling not just the defeat of her special weekend, but the profound embarrassment of having collapsed on the first major deal after Max's, a crucial link in the deal-chain of the team's survival.

She coded an outside line and started to dial Sven in Copenhagen. As she waited for the line to answer, she lit a Gaullois and started to cry.

The Rooftop, appropriately named, perched itself on an

architectural needle at the fringe of the West End and flashed its boogie beacon across the slumbering city seven days a week. For Sirkka it had recently become a kind of second living room, a den full of din where she could hide from her weariness and watch others – usually younger, fitter and happier – rave with the dawn. When she wasn't travelling (which was infrequently: she had made seven New York trips in five weeks, three to Sven in Denmark, one to Tokyo), it was here she came to dine and deliberate and question what she was doing so consistently and so desperately wrong.

From childhood she had craved adventure, excitement, travel to exotic places. Growing up in a strict Finnish household, she had controlled her quixotic impulses but kept the flame alive.

At twenty her work with the UN blended academic flair with that penchant for adventure. Her journeys through Africa and the Middle East were enchanting – but not fulfilling. Something was missing. A career leap into banking seemed to provide the answer. Here was adrenalin, a real jungle of spiritual dangers that outpaced even mortal threat. Here was excitement to answer her untypical Finnish passion! Here was all she wanted, but it was still not enough. Above her bed, back in the glamorously dull apartment behind Harrods, was a plaque with the words: *It is better to travel hopefully than to arrive.* Sven had given it to her, teasingly, on the occasion of their first seriously missed date, that time when her plane had been fog-bound for half a day at JFK. Now, often, she thought about that plaque and those words. At Shane Longman she had what she had always desired: she had excitement, she travelled. But wasn't this the irony? Her travelling *was* her arrival. She was where she always tactically aimed to be: in the clouds, with her feet rarely touching the ground; it was everything she had ever wanted, but it simply wasn't fun any more.

Sirkka called for Dave, her favourite barman, and demanded a Smirnoff, blue. When she saw him prop the glass she shouted in alarm, 'Not a glass, Dave. The bottle. I intend to be here for a while.'

'Do you want the menu?'

'I'm on a diet, Dave.'

The barman hissed disapproval and reluctantly gave the lovely lady the tall neat bottle. The speaker at her ear barked out Robert Palmer demanding better lovin' and she thought hotly about Sven, about her sugary pleas – '*Jeg hadet meget katastrophie her . . . Na jeg skal komme neste uke-end*' – and his bland, fading-interest responses. At the end of their conversation she had the positive impression that he was glad she couldn't make it and she said so and he replied that since their communications were so bad it would be just as well if they skipped seeing each other for a bit. She had been crying insanely throughout, for no clear reason really, but she hid it from him. She told him she loved him, but he didn't give the usual reflex reaction. He just said a kind of 'see you soon' and it crushed her. The familiarity of the Rooftop saved her life, because she had not been in control when the call ended and the eruption of her emotions scared her.

A Kir, a couple of dry Martinis and now a vodka: that was the sure prescribed medication. Already her nerves had stabilized; in an hour or two she might even be dancing.

A voice boomed at her shoulder, a voice she knew: 'Some celebration, Sirkka. This deal they're talking about must really be a cracker!'

Jimmy Destry slid onto the seat beside her and

poured himself a measure of her Smirnoff. The weekend was nigh, the trading machinery was idling, it was
time for fun. Jimmy was pressed, starched and ready
for all-comers. He eyed the dancing talent all around
and babbled on, not seeing Sirkka's pain: 'Got a lot
ahead for the weekend. Chas, me and Louise – did he
tell you about this gal Louise? Nice kid – we're finalizing
our shopping for the house. Furniture, at long last.
She's some kid. She's changed the place from top to
bottom. And, man, can she cook. I tell you, I've had
some pizzas Egon Ronay would rave about . . .' He
suddenly saw her anguish, and the hazy focus of her
eyes. He stopped dead.

'The deal blew. Ari, my angel, pulled out.' She bit her
drink. 'That bastard. That lousy, unconditional bastard.'

'I thought it was in the can – ?' he started dumbly.

'For God's sake, Jimmy!' she cursed. 'I *have to* get it
back on the rails. Some way.'

'Why don't you let me take you home?'

He touched her arm and she rocked savagely away
from him. 'I can take myself home! What do you think
I am!' She went for the vodka but he got to it first.

'Come on, Sirkka. You've nearly emptied this. What's
the point in killing yourself because one deal blows up?'

'I'm not going, Jimmy, and don't preach to me. You
of all people.'

He watched her drain her drink, and dribble, and
give a little nervous shake. He boldly took her arm.
'Come on, we're going to fix that deal. If I can
help – ?'

'*Ari!*'

The word came out like a cannon shot and blood
drained from Sirkka's face.

Jimmy rose beside her and turned to follow her line
of vision. Yes, it was the hook-nosed Greek he knew,

steering through the tables fifteen yards away, an interesting blonde locked on his arm. The Greek was laughing, then he suddenly looked in their direction, blinked very fast, and stalled. In a split-second he decided to go forward and brave it. He approached the bar.

Sirkka's voice was now very strange. She spoke in short sentences that returned the Finnish accent she so conscientiously suppressed: 'Aristotle, you arrogant Greek pimp! You screwed up my deal. You messed up my weekend. You're screwing up my life!'

Warning lights flashed in Sirkka's eyes and Jimmy took a firm hold of her upper arm. 'Don't overdo it, Sirkka. It's history.'

'*He's* about to be history!' She stuck a finger hard into Ari's ribs. 'I bailed you out of a jam. Me and Chas, remember? You called him trying to get rid of those Austrian notes. We obliged. And now you stick me just as the market closes.'

The Greek showed a row of glittering white teeth. 'It was unavoidable. When I reconsidered my financial outlay – '

'Just as the market closed!'

'That was mere coincidence.'

'Really? Well, let's say it's just destiny that your blonde tart led you into the lion's den tonight. Someone should have told you it was dangerous.'

Without notice Sirkka swung out with a balled fist, catching the Greek under the eye. He crashed back over a stool and cracked his arm against a falling table. Diners screamed and the DJ on his chrome perch signalled to some beefy bouncers decorating the alcoves. The bouncers pushed forward through the dancing crowd but they were still yards away from Sirkka when she grabbed the vodka bottle and smashed it against the bar. Ari scrambled backwards on the heels of his hands, a half-moon cut bubbling blood on his right cheek. Sirkka swooped, but Jimmy clasped her hard round the waist and Dave vaulted the bar in a split-second. Dave blocked the bouncers, who were cursing threateningly.

'I'll cut him in two,' Sirkka was swearing. 'Just let me go!'

Jimmy swivelled her and slapped her face gently. 'Sirkka, for God's sake! Get a grip on yourself. You'll regret this. Put the bottle down. Now, Sirkka!'

The pallor of her face was startling, like a doll's, and her eyes began to roll in her head. 'Get the police,' someone shouted but Jimmy tore the bottle from her hand and passed it to Dave. 'Get her out of here, man,' Dave urged, and he leaned down to help Ari to his feet.

The Greek was still in shock but he regained himself to point a fist at Jimmy. 'You'd better tell her about the law, friend. I've a mind to take an action against her. That was a criminal assault.'

'We thought maybe someone should go over to make sure she's OK,' Chas said.

'So why doesn't one of you go over?'

Declan faced his surprise visitors, Jimmy and Chas, and contained an exasperated sigh. It was late, he was tired, Michelle hung heavy on him. He just wanted to kick off his shoes, flop on the couch, take in some more Sinatra. All he ever seemed to listen to nowadays was Sinatra, but for some strange reason the needle on his player seemed too often to find that same groove, 'The Gal That Got Away'.

'I got her home,' Jimmy said, 'but she wasn't in good shape. I called to make sure she was OK, but she's not answering – '

'I haven't got a car,' Declan said testily. 'The Audi's dodgy again – '

'I'll drive you,' Chas jumped in. 'No problem.'

It was a drag, an uprooting, an evening's end he didn't want, but as Declan stomped to the bathroom and washed his face and pulled on a fresh shirt he thought of Sirkka, of how once their friendship had been a rock and a beacon for him, of how much he fundamentally cared for her. Jimmy said the Ari deal was a mess, and Sirkka had exploded at the Greek in a physical attack. Declan frowned at his reflection in the mirror. Yes, he had dues to pay. Not just because he liked her, but because part of her deal was on his recommendation.

In the street it was raining, a pumping flood that rushed up from the gutters. Declan sat silent beside Chas and half-listened as the young traders swapped tales of the wondrous Louise and how her presence had transformed their bachelor lives.

At Sirkka's apartment Declan asked them to join him but Jimmy was adamant – he had done his good deed for the day; now it was Declan's turn. 'If you want us, you'll find us at the Rooftop.'

Declan used his old key – emblem of an old lifestyle, a different dream – and let himself into Sirkka's hall. A discarded pair of fine nylon stockings lay on the floor and as he stooped to pick them up her voice thundered down on him: 'What the hell are you doing here?'

'I came to see if you were OK.'

'How did you get in?'

He held up the key. 'I really just wanted to make sure my furniture was OK. Remember, I bought most of it.'

'I want that key back. You really have no right . . .' She ranted on, every word charged with an anger that belonged somewhere else. He took it calmly, settling himself in a chair till the fury had abated, knowing her like he knew her.

When the rage was spent she offered him a drink and filled one herself. It struck him, knowing her, that she had drunk herself through drunkenness to a shaky sobriety. She threw herself in a chair opposite him and said, 'Well, you've seen the peep show. You can tell I'm OK.' And then, gently, 'Thanks for coming over.'

'I'm so terribly sorry about recommending Ari. I never thought he was the kind of guy to double back.'

'Can you save me, Declan?'

Declan imagined Ansen's anger, the weekend hopes. 'Leon in Tokyo might be an answer.'

'Yes, dammit, let me try him!'

Coffee seemed like a sensible idea. As she jumped at the phone he went into the kitchen he knew so well and brewed whatever he found and threw in a half dozen spoonfuls of sugar crystals. She would quaff it and be ill and it would do her good. In an hour she would be lost in the bliss of sleep, her agonies over.

When he returned to the lounge she was pacing hotly, the phone cradled on her shoulder. The object of her wrath was now Leon, the friendliest, ablest Shane dealer in Tokyo: 'For God's sake, Leon, there must be a client you play golf with? A pension fund that wants to expand? A home investor trying to spread his wings? Everyone wants Europe today. You said so yourself . . .' She listened, screwed the cushion in her lap into a fierce ball, then exploded once more. 'Dammit, there is no up-side! I'm in a corner and you know it. Harry isn't the kind of man who forgets. I set up my end fine, it wasn't my fault some crook backed out . . .' She stopped a moment, her face becoming taut as a drum. 'Don't give me this crap, Leon. So he didn't actually buy! So I should have had the deal written in stone! Come on, that's not how the trade goes and you know it!' Leon apparently did not know it. She cursed him. 'Screw yourself, asshole!' and the phone went down with a crash.

At the tail end of the rage Declan slipped into the bathroom and took some Valium from her press. He pushed the coffee into her hand and made her drink it and, as he guessed, she rushed out to be sick. When she returned he gave her the Valium and watched her wash it down with Perrier. She curled up in a ball in the wicker swing-chair and rocked herself. 'Some life. V's to build your ego, friends to stab you in the back.'

'Don't feel sorry for yourself, Sirkka. It's valueless. Tell yourself you messed it and get it right next time. OK, my advice was bad – but Leon is right. You shouldn't pitch Harry until you have the chit. This is an unforgiving town.'

'All of a sudden you're wise.'

'Not exactly all of a sudden. I've been twenty-something years refining the process.'

'Sit by me. I want to see if those hazel specks are still in your eyes.'

He sat on a bean cushion four feet from her and held the wicker cradle and rocked her. 'Give me one of your wise quotations, Declan. Remember how we laughed? You had an answer for everything.'

He mused. 'All right, let's see. Oh yes. How about this one: there's no law that says you have to be miserable.'

'An original, right? From the wisdom file of the new Declan?'

'Not exactly. Harry Morgan. Hemingway, more or less. You see, I'm really just the same old Declan.'

Her gaze became introspective. 'I'm the one who's

changed. I remember my days in Juba. The people were wonderfully . . . real. Primitive values, we might say. But I loved them. I loved the honesty that underlay everything. Basic things meant everything. Rainfall was a wondrous miracle, a marriage was a cause for joy.' She refocussed on him wryly. 'What a tangled web we weave, eh, Declan?'

Her eyes became misty tired and he rocked her more. 'I can make some calls,' he said. 'Some old school chums, that sort of thing. You never know – ' He was smiling with all the reassurance he could muster.

'Oh why is everything such a mess for me?'

'Nonsense.'

'No, it's true. Sven and I – it's falling apart. I try to pretend it's fine by staying away. And then I wonder why it isn't fine when we're together. My work, my life, it's all a ruin. The most significant object in my world is a microwave oven.'

The comedy of the tragedy made Declan smile. 'I think you must sleep – '

'God, I'm unhappy. I'm fed up with being unhappy. I'm fed up with being under pressure. I'm fed up with pretending to be tough. I don't even like myself.'

He was calm and firm: 'You need sleep.'

'Sleep with me.'

There was no surprise and no confusion. He rocked her and looked at her and thought; we're in the same boat, really. Birds with a wing down. Tired of pretending and seriously lacking love.

'I snore,' he said. But she didn't reply. She was already asleep.

NINE

Wisdom

On Saturday, a day of glorious autumnal softness, Leonard Ansen cabbed to Richmond Golf Club to participate in the Cancer Charity Pro-Am, as he'd promised to months before. He felt good because he had slept well, replete with the trust, humour and generosity of Peter Longman; but he was edgy at the thought of Lee Wolf's likely presence in the game.

Longman's midnight caution as they split on the Connaught steps rang in his ears: 'Watch Wolf. There's fire in him yet. James Farrell is the spirit of my dad, but he ain't what he used to be. Maybe I'm a fool, Leonard, but I look to you for the survival of my father's pioneering style. Don't be misled. Wolf is on the up. You're hanging in, but that's about all your doing. You need to get him in his place.'

James Fineman's nine o'clock call helped. The lawyer had had a fortuitous and splendid encounter last evening at Le Gavroche: the DTI's Mr Hope, a turning worm. The mood had changed dramatically, Fineman promised. Sworn statements from Ansen's broker and, most importantly, from Hal Lowenstein just returned from Bahrain looked positively like settling concerns. The general feeling was one of regret and embarrassment that the DTI had pursued matters so noisily. Mr Ansen, it was agreed, had impeccable character and many impeccable allies: Mr Lowenstein was prepared to quit the takeover deal rather than see his friend and associate strung up for a few grands' worth of stock.

The clubhouse buzzed with the rosy chatter of a fun day. Wives, girlfriends and tots abounded, hounded here and there by cub reporters from local rags. There was laughter and the clink of happy glasses and tall golf stories. Ansen took a coffee, then changed into his pink Slazengers and white handmade shoes and made for the pro shop to establish his ranking.

An American voice interrupted him: 'Gee, Leonard, you look swell. You know the Bronx joke: golf is the only game where a white dude can dress like a black pimp and get away with it! Ha! Ha!'

It was Wolf, clad in wolfish brown, with a rakish tam o' shanter that was vintage toytown American. Ansen said a pleasant Hello but Wolf wanted more. He put out a fat dry hand. 'Put it here, buddy. The past is a foreign country, I say. What's done is done.' How many stiff whiskies? Ansen wondered. Or was it the serious fear of Longman, the insidious overnight feeling that he had stepped too close to a fatal edge?

They walked in the sunshine together, men at odds, acting with the flair of Oscar-winning actors. 'I need a little of your talent to rub off on me today,' Wolf droned sweetly. 'My short game is the pits. Can't hold the nines, wedges, putts. Think it's because I've too much upper body strength. Football at college overdeveloped me. A great problem in the US. Plus I boxed, did I tell you?'

'I don't take it too seriously,' Ansen said vaguely. 'When I play, I play.'

'And when you work, you work. Good philosophy. That's obviously what makes you bounce back. I'm damned if you don't have a capacity to go on bouncing, Leonard. I have to hand it to you. I mean, I thought when so many deals went west you and your boys and gals would call it a day. I see old Denzil Mason here today. Pacific Pension Fund. You guys blew him out, didn't you? Who was it lost that account? Jimmy Destry – or McConnochie?'

'Jimmy. It was unfortunate.'

'And I heard Sirkka had trouble last night?'

Ansen blocked the doorway of the pro shop and faced Wolf. 'Lee, I'm going to be rude again. I came here to play, not to do some laundry.'

Wolf was savage in his reply. 'I know what you mean, Leonard. You need to do a lot of laundry. All that linen needs to be washed. Exhausting. You clearly need a break from the worry of it.'

No more words were spoken. Ansen looked for the announcement board and Wolf disappeared to the sales counter, purchasing tees. Ansen checked his placing and found himself teeing off at midday, partnered in a fourball with two local club pros and an amateur listed as 'TBA' – to be arranged.

At twelve he was climbing the wooden steps to the medal tee when the amateur partner revealed himself – as Hal Lowenstein.

Baked brown from the eastern sun, Lowenstein embraced him hugely, swinging him off his feet. 'I heard the nonsense,' he said. 'I tried to get you yesterday but I was too late. I told the DTI to go take a jump – '

'I know. I'm grateful. I didn't holler for you because I didn't want them to start shouting about conspiracy – '

'To hell with 'em, Leonard. They're wrong on this one, and that's all that matters. Did it do you harm?'

'*Sssssssssssh!*' One of the pros, a wizened ancient who took his game with a biblical intensity, wagged his driver. Ansen and Lowenstein fell silent and the game began.

As the four men followed their drives down the fairway Ansen and his friend fell into step. 'Sure it hurt,' Ansen confessed. 'Smoke goes up and people talk. Lee Wolf made a meal of it. He tried to use it to lever me and the team out. Insider trading, the worst rap anyone can land in the City. Incest, murder, state secrets – they're baby food compared.'

Lowenstein frowned. 'Hmm. It gets interesting.'

'What do you mean?'

'Fineman told me you got your tip from Max Lubin. Who in turn got it from Billy Lang. Who in turn got it from someone who got it from Sean Evans.'

'Billy Lang's the City shoe-shine boy. He's weird and insane – '

'But very dependable and *very* discreet. And here's the rub: Billy, by my information, got word of what Lowenstein was planning from Lee Wolf.'

'Via Sean Evans?'

'That's right. Sean departed from us under a bit of a cloud. He's an expense account pirate, like I always said. But he confessed to me last night that he told Lee Wolf – '

'Who tipped Billy, and Billy being Max's great informer . . . ?'

'That's the way it reads to me.'

Ansen felt like rolling in hysterics on the ground. Instead he just chuckled. His Penfold was perfectly placed, tee'd almost, on a tuft of scutch grass. He took his five iron. 'Max looks out for lines for me,' he said. 'You're aware of that?'

'Yes, and you'd sold the apartment and had cash in hand.'

Ansen blasted the five arrow-straight down the fairway. It hit the lip of the left-hand bunker, jumped eight feet and plonked on the green fifty feet from the cup. He sighed satisfaction. 'My luck is turning.'

'There's a lot you could do with that kind of information, Leonard.'

'Let me file it away. I've got a feeling I'll be needing it before too long.'

They played on, brushed by luck and blessed by supreme weather, and outscored the pros easily. An eagle two at the last hole gave Ansen the best score of the round and a special prize of a weekend trip to Paris, staying at the George V, all expenses paid.

When they returned to the clubhouse it was five thirty and starting to rain. The game behind them, the last of the day, was huddling against a coming storm. Ansen showered and changed feeling giddily high, and then he rejoined Lowenstein at the bar.

Lowenstein called for champagne. 'I feel guilty about your misfortune,' he told Ansen. 'But I think I can help restore your spirits.'

'You've helped already, Hal. And you'll go on helping as Lowenstein's management pushes up my stock.'

'No, something more than that. A legitimate and legal business tip. An introduction. Wait here.'

Ansen waited, intrigued, and Lowenstein returned with an elderly familiar-faced man by his side. Here was a face from the recent past, an expensive face, a coal miner's face, a recollection of failure. Ansen shuffled the jigsaw together and recalled just as the man announced in a rich Rhonda voice, 'Denzil Glynn Mason, you've probably forgotten me?'

'No indeed.' Ansen thought of Jimmy, of the messed-up account that cost so dearly. Pacific Pension, one of the heftiest in the land, a shrewd and conservative investor whose fingers had been burned by Shane Longman six months ago. 'I suspect you wish you could forget Shane.'

The Welshman gave an economic smile. 'Hal persuades me otherwise. He says mistakes are the best commendations. Or rather, how people try to make amends. Those who don't make mistakes, or don't admit to them, don't try to improve, if you get my meaning?'

'Yes, sir, I do.'

The 'sir' helped. Denzil Mason appeared suddenly relaxed. He spotted the champagne before Ansen, pushed it aside and called for three beers. 'I liked your eight iron on the last, laddie – '

'It was a nine.'

'Better. You're strong. You must be to push a driver three fifty yards up that bugger of a hole. Get this brown stuff into you. Much better than that Cinderella crap.'

Ansen accepted the beer with dutiful thanks. Lowenstein pulled a face as he sucked reluctantly at his, but he winked optimistically at Ansen.

'Let me ask you a question, boyo. Guilders. I want your opinion.'

Ansen didn't hesitate. 'Over-valued in the EMS, is my opinion.'

The big Welshman found a cigar in his inside pocket, broke it in half and offered part to Ansen. Ansen accepted, took a book of matches from the ashtray and lit for both of them.

'The Pacific Pension Fund wants to move out of guilders. How does that strike you?'

'Sensible. And a very attractive proposition, from my point of view.'

Mason's smile was more generous. 'All right. Monday I want you to talk to my partner Ted Trelaunay. Bring your best man this time. None of that snotty-nosed rubbish – '

'You'll get someone special, I assure you.'

The men shook hands and from the tail of his eye Ansen saw Lee Wolf drip and shake his way into the clubhouse bar. He'd been caught in the rain, and rained out. Commiserations were loud and the facts bellowed out: his score was high, his game was lost, he stood before all, a soggy and dejected loser.

Across the bar their eyes briefly met. Each took in the other's situation and the rules of engagement were in an instant rewritten.

Waking with a woman is as telling as sleeping with her. The subdued emotions of soporific wakefulness are truer, untainted by the guile of conquest. This was Declan's experience, and it was his habit to linger beside a lady friend when he woke with her, and assess.

But he did not linger with Sirkka. They woke late, near two thirty, and her stirring movement drove him from the bed to the shower, and from there to the telephone.

It was three and the unseasonal rain was again hammering the windows when she came into the lounge and found him badgering down the phone. Her head was dull and muddled after the booze and Valium but she was calm and keen with hunger. She signalled that she would fry up some eggs and went into the kitchen. Minutes later he came in, fussily ignoring her state of nudity. She laughed at him. 'Don't worry, it's not a seduction ploy to pull you back to bed. We Finns are naked all the time! It's our splendid bracing climate, you see.'

'I have to leave you,' he said. 'Hudson needs me.'

'A regular visiting psychiatric service, eh, Declan?'

He observed his own coldness, the distance he was trying to maintain. He walked to her and embraced her and she felt small and, yes, bird-like in his arms. She kissed him, and he responded without thinking, allowing her tongue to probe.

When they broke he said, 'I've been labouring hard for you. I made calls to old chums and begged a bit. Problem is, no one wants a deal this size without time to ruminate and study the options. It has no miracle grab-line, it's a cold tough sell.'

'What about the American end? Assuming *someone* wants it over there, someone must be attracted here.'

'I'll keep on hustling, Sirkka, don't doubt that.'

'What's Hudson's trouble?'

'I don't know. I rang home to check my answer machine and he'd left a message. From last night, looking for an urgent chat. Some domestic drama, by the sounds of it. I'll get a taxi over.'

She held him again at the front door, carelessly nude, 'Who gives a damn!' He shifted uneasily but let it happen. 'Tomorrow's dinner party at Max's,' she cajoled. 'Will you make me your date?'

'Sirkka, listen to me – '

But she blocked his lips with a finger. 'I'm not asking for your hand in wedlock, Declan. I'm a big girl, plus I know you're in love with Michelle.' He narrowed a gaze at her. 'Don't be dumb, Declan. It's written all over you. Console yourself with this thought: her German boyfriend wanted her to stay, but she ran to get away from him. That's what New York was all about for her. Escaping from the wrong man.'

This gush was bewildering, he'd never known of any conversational intimacy between Michelle and Sirkka; on the contrary, there was always restraint, maybe even suspicion and jealousy.

'Thank you,' was all he could think of saying.

'You could go after her.' She stalled. 'I'll rephrase it: you should go after her. If you really want her.'

'I'm too young.' He touched his forehead. 'Up here. Maybe in a while – '

'Don't leave it too long. Life is a while.' She hugged him tight. 'It is good to be with you, Declan. Just to remember what it was like for a starry weekend all those centuries ago.'

He kissed her cheek, faintly disoriented by her caring, faintly embarrassed by his relative indifference. 'I'll call you in the morning and pick you up mid-afternoon. Provided my cantankerous motor allows, that is. In the meantime, you get more rest. And keep off the booze.'

'If I lose this deal I'm out.'

'Balls. Leonard won't stand by and – '

'No, I mean I'm out by my own decision, Declan. If I can't cut the important ones I should be out to pasture. Maybe back where I truly belong, in the green fields of Africa.'

He left her with leaden thoughts and (she insisted he borrow her car) drove in a hurry towards Hudson's, thinking gratefully of his busyness, that the dash of the days gave him little time to imagine Michelle packing and preparing and biding adieu to the temporary London life. Once, caught in traffic, a song they joked was 'their song' came on the radio. It was a rusty classic – 'Theme from a Summer Place' – which she said reminded her of winters in Northern Europe, her growing up on frozen lakes, and skiing, and wondering about *real* summers.

Absurd, but he wanted to cry. But then the lights changed and someone trumped the horn and he was back in today and lane-skipping to catch Hudson fast.

At Highgate Hudson was running down the steps as he drove up. He looked twice as he saw Hudson swing a hatchet at a doddery signpost that announced: 'For Sale – Costello, Glennon and O'Neill, agents'.

'You're selling?' Declan poked his head out into the rain. 'I thought this was your castle and mausoleum?'

'The hell I'm selling! She's whipping it from under me. Alex! I gave them twenty-four hours to remove these signs, I've had enough.'

Declan pushed Hudson out of the rain, into the ornate and suddenly sad hallway. Their voices pitched and clashed and the unseen nanny in the bowels of the house shouted for silence. 'The baby is restless, for heaven's sake!'

Hudson immediately calmed. 'I can't believe it, but she's doing it. I called the estate agents. I had to drag it out of them. She insisted the house was hers to sell – '

'Costello, Glennon, O'Neill?'

'Yes, I know you know them.'

'I played rugby with Glennon. I knew his sister Renée – '

'That's why I called. They won't give me her address. I tried everyone I could think of. I tried that goddam agency in Paris but they deny she ever came there.'

'That's interesting, Hudson. Seriously.'

'Will you call your man? Find out?'

'We'll drive over.'

They went in Sirkka's car and Hudson insisted on tackling them himself. He launched out at Glennon, emphatically demanding that the sales brochures be destroyed and all references removed from the books. 'How the hell can you advertise the property when you haven't even seen the inside of it?' he slammed.

Glennon tried to be polite. 'We have seen the inside of it. Five years ago we sold it for a client. Mrs Talbot has since given us a full account of the alterations, including this – ' He proferred the architect's structural revision plans.

'She's in town! Where is she?' Hudson could contain himself no longer. He snatched the address and strode out. 'How can she do this?' he said in a smouldering loaded voice. 'Forget me, but what about the kid? The kid needs a home. I can live with her setting fire to my dreams. I can live with her destroying the house I gave everything for. But I cannot accept this. This is barbarous. I said she was as good as dead before – but now I mean it.' His voice was utterly without feeling: 'How can a man go from caring so much, from loving the ground a woman walks on, to this? This hatred.'

They drove across London in silence, towards the West London address Hudson had procured.

It was a tall Victorian house. The rain continued relentlessly.

'I'll come with you,' Declan said.

'No. Wait.'

Hudson rang the rusted bell of number seven. He was sweating, his fists rolled tight by his sides. The door opened and a timid-looking old woman blinked out and smiled, her eyes flicking up to the sky. 'Once it rained on Swithin's I knew it would rain all year. We must be thankful for these little respites.'

'My name is Talbot,' Hudson said quickly. 'I am looking for – '

'Oh yes, dear, Alex. But you won't find her today. She only stays when she's seeing Dr Morris. A couple of days at a time, that's all.'

'Dr Morris?'

'The psychiatrist, dear. We help him out with accommodation for his patients.'

The fire spat and sparkled in the Adam fireplace and the whisky glowed gold in the fine Burano tumblers. Upstairs the baby dreamed his baby dreams, down here Hudson and Declan tussled with the affairs of men.

They sat on opposite sides of the big fireplace, concentration locked in the flames. 'Morris wouldn't yield?' Declan asked.

'Doctors don't. He said I could make an appointment through his secretary on Monday in the formal way. He wouldn't discuss Alex. Just said he'd pass on my message.'

'At least you know she'll be there again in a week or so – '

'I can't believe it,' Hudson mumbled for the hundredth time. He swigged whisky. 'Alex. All my stupid suspicions, thinking she just wanted to dump me and get back to her career. All I ever thought of was how strong she was. She never showed any emotion.' He stopped and thought long and hard then he said, 'You know, that's what breaks me up: the fact that I couldn't get in to her emotions.' He gave a humourless laugh. 'Ironic. Talking with you like this. It's the only time I've ever really *discussed* the way it was. Certainly Alex didn't want me to analyse it.'

'Do you ask yourself why?'

'There's something behind that question.'

'Yes, you're right. Us. Shane Longman. The way we are. The single-mindedness that makes us succeed. We're a particular breed, don't you think. Deeply selfish, tunnel-visioned. You're hot, Hudson, one of the best in town. You earn that reputation. You work your butt off. But it sometimes makes you – and me and all the rest of us – dull boys. Worse. It makes us hard boys. *We* are the tough cookies. The automatons.'

Hudson reached for the whisky but Declan edged it away. He laughed inwardly at his sanctimonious gesture, then became serious again: 'Do you ever ask yourself how much she missed working?'

Hudson shrugged. 'She wanted that baby.'

'Good answer. Do you ever ask yourself how much she missed *you*?'

Hudson looked deep, deep into Declan's face. 'You're old beyond your years, Declan. Did anyone ever tell you that?'

'I've had a lot of experience in draughty bedsits and plush hotel suites.' He back-stepped. 'She loved you, Hudson. Probably still loves you very much. Don't make the mistake of closing the book on her and blaming her and hating her for selling the house under you. Give her a chance.'

'How, Declan? By sitting here and waiting for her?'

'Life doesn't read like an eternal New Testament. Sometimes the miracles are slow in coming. Give it time.'

They poured some small final whiskies and downed them and then Declan took his coat and went out into the moist chill night.

TEN

A Leap
in the Dark

Max readied himself for a celebration party that Hudson promised would be a Dickensian feast. Ceremony was Max's forte. He adored all the rituals of linen-pressing and table-setting and candle-placing and flower-arranging. Doubly so when the cause for celebration was significantly, in part at least, him.

He was up before midday (Sunday was his traditional day of sloth: he'd seen just one Sunday morning in two years) and supervising his visiting cleaners with fascistic glee. The meal, he decided, would be served at the baronial table in the Gothic hall. Accordingly, hallway furniture was rolled aside and brass side tables for pretzels and punch were lined against the walls. From the garden he clipped clumps of alstroemeria, gloxinia and Michaelmas daisies; these he mixed with the armfuls of carnations delivered from the local flower dealers the evening before.

By mid-afternoon the house was fit for a visiting king,

a vivid vision of colour and cockeyed charm, perfumed from paradise. Max showered and pulled on his favourite oddball Gaultier suit, then slipped the Dior clip (actually a woman's, and a gift from Wendy) into his pigtail. He looked good, good enough for Gershwin, so he plugged the music system into the 'open house' mode and waltzed down the golden stairway to the strains of *'Allegro ben ritmato e deciso'*.

In the kitchen it struck him suddenly that the stage was set but the play was absent: no food was yet prepared. And there was no sign of Hudson.

Wendy rang. 'All set, Max?'

'Well, after a fashion. We're running a bit, er, late. I said five thirty, but make it six thirty. Have you got your date set?'

'No. I'm a lonely lady tonight, but I'm not worried. I'm among friends.' She paused. 'I hope. Who else is coming?'

'Everyone who counts. Declan. Hannah. Sirkka. You. Chas and his girl. Jimmy.'

'And most importantly Hudson, surely?'

'Oh him. Well of course him. He'll arrive.'

Wendy detected a note of incipient panic and played cruelly on it: 'I don't know, he's been acting odd lately – ' She heard Max choke. 'I'll bet he doesn't show. But I suppose we can send out for fries?'

Hudson showed. But this was sub-par Hudson, loosely interested but distinctly distracted. He carried parcels of food and made a grumbling effort to suggest enthusiasm, but Max saw through it.

'Look at your tie,' Max complained, wiping baby food from the otherwise immaculate silk. The questions he wanted to be asking rose in his throat, but he held them back. 'Get yourself organized, man! We have a dozen mouths to feed in a couple of hours! Now let's have the menu.'

In the kitchen Hudson grimly began the preparation for the meal: it would be 'Turkey Farci a l'Orange', an exotic spicy stuffing, and Bigarade sauce, set up by a starter of 'Coquilles St Jacques Hongroise', a buttery scallops dish. 'It's my Thanksgiving speciality,' Hudson said lifelessly. 'Designed for duck but rejigged to fit the cross-cultural divide.'

'Instruct me,' Max offered.

Side by side they set to work on the turkey and fish, remotely silent from one another. Finally Max broke: 'There's no point my pretending. I know you've located Alex. Declan told me. You don't have to pour it all out, but I just want to say if you need a gentle ear . . .'

'I'm numb, Max. All the assumptions I made – ' His voice dried up and Max poured him a glass of cooking plonk. 'I had it built up in my mind: her in Paris. All the wild imaginings one goes through. But it seems it's not like that. She's . . . she's in therapy.'

'What separates the sexes is a common language. It's the old story, Hudson. Two people see things differently.'

'But how can we fix it if she won't meet me?'

Max screwed up his face in concentration, preparing the pronouncement that would solve all ills. Hudson paused to study him . . . and then the electricity cut out.

The chaos that followed drove Max to his knees. The food had barely hit the oven. The music scrawled and died. Hudson stumbled and fell in the darkness, injuring himself.

'For God's sake,' Hudson screamed from the abyss, 'the food is destroyed unless I get heat now! Is this a joke?'

But the power was out to stay. A call to the local electricity service explained the problem: there had been an accident, power lines had fallen, nothing could be done for several hours.

Hudson flew a litany of American swear words. 'Shouldn't we get on the blower and call everyone?' he demanded. 'Right now before it's too late? Cancel it!'

'Christ, this isn't like you at all!' Max shouted him down. 'Relax . . . and anyway, it's a little too late to reverse things.'

A hammering at the door heralded the arrival of the first of the guests. Wendy Foley was followed by Chas and Louise, and Jimmy, and then Declan and Sirkka. Wendy looked better than Max ever remembered her, her hair in a soft chignon from which errant tails looped sexily, her Katharine Hamnett frock accentuating a body full of muscular youth.

In the thickening murk, Max and Hudson lamented aloud but Declan and Wendy refused to let the mood slide. Declan called for all the available candles and Wendy found some phone books to seek out the best nearby takeaways. 'In the spirit of good traders,' she said, 'let's trade. If we can't have a glorious beano, let's have something exotic and atmospheric and – '

'Weird,' Jimmy Destry suggested. 'I'll have the king prawns in toad sauce.'

In the absence of a doorbell a thumping knock sounded and Declan took a candle and went to the hall door. He opened it and lifted the candle and saw the flickering light on the faces of Michelle and Bruno. It was a dream, he told himself: this hazy, half-lit world, the thunderous confusion of the background – and *her*.

'Hello, Declan. I tried calling you last night.'

'I thought you'd be busy with travel tags and everything?'

Bruno was no longer smiling. Even in the dim light Declan could see the piercing antagonism and somehow, brilliantly, it cheered him. She was fleeing to New York to escape him, that was true. But this antagonism was directed at Declan. Could it be that she'd spoken to Bruno about Declan? That she'd confessed to a friendship that bordered on . . . ? He held himself in check.

'Not going to invite us in?' Michelle said. 'It's creepy out here without any drive lights.'

Everything about Declan's evening altered then. This was no longer another rambling knees-up; it was a critical evening *with her*. Max and Hudson needed help in the kitchen, but Declan's mind raced to take the challenge of the opportunity. There was a lot he wanted to say to her, given half a chance. A lot of last stones to be turned – and apologies to be made.

In the kitchen Hudson had blundered retrieving the sauce pan and its contents were everywhere. Declan knuckled down to helping mop up the mess but Sirkka saw his restlessness. On hands and knees alongside him she whispered, 'You are still my date, I hope?' The bite of jealousy in her tone made him recoil and squint through the dark at her.

He struggled to keep the agitation from his voice. 'I'm not that shallow, you know.'

'She looks just wonderful. Even in the dark she glows.'

'I didn't notice.'

'I did.'

'Let's change the subject. Leon – ?'

'Leon, Lewis . . . Declan, forget it. The book is closed.'

'Maybe – '

She snapped, 'I said forget it.' And then she softened, and held his arm. 'I'm sorry. Finnish manners. You've been wonderful. But I have to accept the way it is now. Here, give me the mop. Go out and chat to Wendy.' She sucked air. 'Or Michelle.'

He obeyed, washed his hands in the dark and found a candle to guide him back to the big hall. Michelle was there, seated on the confidante, chatting quietly to Chas. Chas looked at Declan, understood, and melted away.

Declan sat uncomfortably, his eyes raking the darkness for Bruno. His hunted look made Michelle chuckle. 'Don't look so scared,' she said. 'You'll start me off again! This reminds me of a film I saw once on late night telly. *The Haunted Palace*, or something. How *does* Max live here?' She peered up at the grey ghostly dome of a ceiling. 'And what about that monstrosity!'

'This place is Max's museum. A museum to vanity, he calls it. I suppose a man – or a woman – likes to see tangible results for years of hard labour. It's important to come out of it with something to show . . .' His words wound down and he thrilled to her piercing, questing stare.

In a low, low voice laced with concern she said, 'Are you all right?'

'Why shouldn't I be?'

'Lately you always look . . . tired out.'

'There've been some problems. Hudson, Sirkka, lots of niggly bits and pieces, forget them.'

'Sirkka. I was once very jealous of her.'

He wanted to scream in her face: *don't do this to me. Don't play games and pretend it's not happening. Don't pretend you don't know!* But he just said, 'There was never much between Sirkka and me other than, well, keeping each other company. I do respect her a lot and I think she's over-stretched at Shane. Her ambitions are all confused but she's got more energy than she knows what to do with, so she keeps on hauling away – '

'That's very sensitive of you.'

'What is?'

'To get involved. Chas told me Sirkka confided that you'd been a tower of strength over the weekend.'

'I had to keep busy.'

'Did you?'

'Well – ' And he was thinking, *now is the time, let her have a last soul-bearing blast; give her everything but, in fairness, expect nothing*. He started to resume but the words wouldn't come: 'I reckoned you and I were pals and . . . I thought to myself, if I don't see her again . . . in friendship one has a responsibility . . .'

'I really wanted you at dinner with Bruno and me the other night.'

He drew back in surprise. 'I'm sorry I was rude to you. In your eager dash to get away to New York – '

'Is that what you think?'

His heartbeat bounced. 'I'm sorry, I . . . you said Bruno didn't want you to go to New York and I sort of assumed – '

'You thought I was running away to New York to avoid Bruno, is that it?'

The sharp edge of criticism in her voice crushed Declan's spirit but all of a sudden Wendy was pulling his arm. She wanted a word with him. She began by babbling on about Shane and the improvement of the team situation with Peter Longman's active support and Declan switched off his mind until suddenly she was speaking his name and the word 'failure' in worrying proximity: '. . . to make sure I see an improvement. Leonard is committed to that too. Now don't take that the wrong way. Our commitment means we do still believe in you. But you've been back-pedalling. So the

Pacific Pension exchange is your chance to make good . . .' She went on to outline the arrangement for tomorrow's meeting with Denzil Mason and Ted Trelaunay, concluding, 'Anyway, Leonard felt you need cheering up. Swinging the right tough deal will do it.'

He smiled at her in the dark. 'Do you think Michelle and that guy Bruno look right together?'

'If you're asking are they happy and suited I'd say . . .' She reflected: 'Yes. It's that particular Aryan temperament. A kind of seriousness, I think.' She saw his gloom. 'Put it out of your head, Declan. You two would never work out. It would end in misery.' She grinned remorselessly. 'Anyway, Bruno's much too tall for you.'

'Tread easy, for you tread on my dreams.'

The tone of her voice changed, became motherly and stern. 'Declan, you must face up. Taking an attitude is the trick. Shut off. Remember Churchill's trick: imagine the written blackboard, all your many problems in scribbled detail. And then wipe it, wipe it clean. You try that. Because it will keep you sane and allow you to get on with your life.'

'You're talking from experience, right?'

'I've been putting a lot of time and thought into relationships lately. I've come to the conclusion that the great trouble is that people mostly don't. They take issues like love too lightly. A one night stand sounds like a lot of fun but where does it lead? I'm not talking about social diseases and all that. I'm talking about crossing the border and finding oneself attached. The responsibilities of emotional engagement. People should focus more on these issues – especially people living the pressure-pot existence of business or politics or – '

'You're lecturing, Wendy.

She pulled a face. 'Dammit, you're right. Call it the consolation factor. Since I've persuaded myself not to live out the melodramas, at least I can preach about them.'

'So Howard is not the man for you?'

She took time before replying. 'No, he's not. I have yet to find the man for me.' She looked at him. 'And you?'

He took a long minute and said, 'Howard's not right for me either.'

'*Touché*!'

The Chinese food had arrived and they were summoned to join the others.

They sat in the dark, clustered and mottled by candlelight, like a Rembrandt painting. Max demanded music – his evening might be down but it would not, emphatically, be *out* – so Jimmy Destry found a battery cassette player and they swung to the sophisticated hysteria of Bon Jovi. 'Is that *all* you have?' Max demanded, mourning his CDs-only collection, but Jimmy just shrugged and stayed in the groove.

'I've got some great Rubinstein,' Wendy offered, but I keep it in the office. The best I can give you is ethnic Cantonese music?'

'Bon Jovi can grow on you,' Chas politely intoned.

Hudson spread out the fragrant packaged feast: fat helpings of yu lang chi, prawns chow mein, stir fried crab laced with ginger and shallots. He dipped a finger of bread into the sherry-soy side dip and moaned, 'God, what we're missing! A thousand million Chinese and they tolerate this garbage. It never ceases to amaze me why they don't rise up and revolt. Obviously their diet keeps them weak and submissive . . .'

Declan sat uncomfortably. Two empty chairs faced him across the table: Bruno and Michelle. He'd seen them in the glass annex where Max grew his strawberries and tomatoes, a candle between them, locked in sincere conversation. As he watched, and tried not to watch, Bruno had reached out and held her face in the palm of his hand, lovingly, and she had tilted her head to respond – or had she? It was impossible, of course, for him to dally and look; also, it was not his business, he had no right. But that didn't stop the ache, felt unbearably now, as the last hours drew on. How had she resolved the matter of Bruno's discomfort with New York? Would he accompany her after all? Or was she slowly disengaging herself from a relationship that was spent?

At last they came in, just as Hudson ladled out the main helping and Max splashed out his finest clarets to kill the taste. Instantly Declan saw their new and glowing contentment, a radiant, sleepy-eyed pleasure like after-sex. He watched Bruno suspiciously, resentfully, but then he saw Wendy's direct challenge and he diverted. Wendy was right. It was all a matter of attitude, and honour. If he cared for Michelle, he must be glad for her happiness.

The table talk had turned, inevitably, to Shane Longman and the City dramas. 'I'm astounded that Ari cheated you,' Chas said to Sirkka. 'Have you been able to recover?'

Wendy was looking critically at Sirkka and Sirkka's depression was absolute: 'I don't care to talk about it any more. It's past tense.'

'But Harry must be livid?' Chas pursued. Jimmy elbowed him and Chas cottoned on, and pulled a face. 'I just wondered . . . what kind of deal it was?'

'Italy Deutschmarks,' Declan put in quietly, then asked for the sherry dip.

'You are moving Italy Deutschmarks?' Bruno said suddenly.

'Everyone responded in surprise, eyes swinging to Bruno, the outsider. But of course he too was involved in banking!

'The deal is two thirds in London, one third in New York,' Sirkka explained dully. 'My London buyer dropped out on Friday. So I'm public enemy number one.' She hesitated. 'Which I suppose is fair.'

'You have been following the elections?'

'What elections?'

'The German Regional Elections, of course.'

'No, I can't say – '

'The Social Democrats have gained a lot of seats.'

The mood at the table was suddenly keen, all eyes fast on Bruno – especially Sirkka's. 'Is that significant?'

'Part of their policy is the imposition of withholding tax on German treasury notes. I would have thought you'd have known about this?'

Hudson, still dreamily lost in Alex, buttered more bread and distributed it, waiter-fashion. He spoke automatically. 'What Bruno means is, if the Social Democrats continue to pick up seats they'll be able to implement their proposed legislation sooner – '

'Shit,' Sirkka barked, striking the table with her fist. 'Why didn't we know about this! Why didn't you tell me, Hudson?'

Hudson recoiled and dropped some bread. 'I knew . . . I thought . . . well, no one consulted me about Italy Deutschmarks.'

'I posted it!' Sirkka half-shouted. 'If you'd kept your eyes open you'd have seen it!'

'Calm down,' Wendy ordered. She addressed Hudson: 'When do these elections close?'

'Saturday. Yesterday.'

'How soon will the results affect the market?' Sirkka rasped.

'Well, it's more the *indication* that affects the market. These are just regional elections. If the Democrats gain a significant number of seats, the Parliament is theirs, the withholding tax goes through and the Euro-Deutschmark becomes flavour of the month.'

'So the market will respond in anticipation of the event?'

'In other words, now,' Hudson agreed.

Sirkka knocked back a big glass of fine claret and her face burned with excitement.

Jimmy proposed a toast to her, then toasted Bruno and it struck Declan as odd that no one mentioned Michelle's imminent departure or offered a celebration toast, least of all Michelle.

Helped by the good and free-flowing wine and driven ever higher by the spirited music, the party ascended. Max became Mad Max once more, pulling Louise onto the floor and recreating the glorious dance steps of the sixties to stubbornly eighties computer-drum beats. Everyone clapped and cheered along.

Declan sat across from Michelle and looked into her pale and peaceful eyes. She smiled at him and he heard himself say, 'Would you like to talk some more?' and she said, warmly, 'Yes, I would.'

They went out to the glasshouse and sat among greenery, lit by a lone candle. It was romantic and unreal and it broke Declan's heart.

'You and Bruno look so happy.'

'We are. Finally. He asked me to marry him.'

'That's . . . terrific.'

'I said I would think it over . . .' she smiled wider, 'in the years to come.'

'I don't understand. He appears so content.'

'We talked. It was the first real talk we've ever shared as adults. Sometimes you know a person so well and so long that you don't see all the little changes. You fix on what you are accustomed to and satisfy yourself that those things go on. And then one day you get a surprise.

'This sounds familiar. Go on.'

'We confessed to each other that our relationship is based on family expectation. I have been running away from him. He has been pursuing me because that's what has been expected. I told him honestly: I was escaping to New York because I didn't want to face up to settling down with him.' *Was* escaping. Declan's heart lifted a mile.

'But he proposed marriage?'

'He is my friend. We have a very deep respect for each other. In a wild and sad world maybe that's enough. He says he could not stand to lose me forever. I assured him he would never lose me by letting me have my freedom. By doing this, he deepens my respect and regard.'

'I see. So . . . New York?' He couldn't look at her.

'I've changed my mind. I'm not going. I think Leonard will understand. I'm going to talk with Wendy now.'

'I . . . see.' He was choked with a schoolboyish emotion. He cleared his throat and turned his face into the shadows to keep his dignity. 'Can I ask you a question? Why did you want me to join you and Bruno at that dinner?'

She stared at him a long time, recapturing his eye. Then she said, 'I suppose I wanted to make a statement to Bruno. I wanted to say, hey, look, there are other men in my life that I am involved with and whom I care about.'

Declan laughed a short laugh. 'You know what I want? I want the night to end right now. This minute. That statement.'

'Then let's be strong.' She stood and he stood into her arms. They held each other, loosely, eyes devouring each twinkling expression. He was home again, he would sleep at night, there was hope.

'I'm sorry for all the grief I have caused you. I'm a very stupid guy most of the time.' He didn't try to kiss her or deepen the embrace. Instead he broke out of her grip and moved towards the door.

'Declan?'

'Yes?'

'It wasn't only Bruno I was running from. I don't have the exclusive franchise on maturity. Sometimes I'm wild and stupid too.'

'I think I understand,' he said and he took her hand and kissed it and they moved back onto the party carousel.

At a quarter to seven in the morning Sirkka was smelling her own sweat and draining the last of the Optrex. She waved to Declan who came through with an angel's step.

'Still at it?' Declan asked, concerned for her. He massaged her shoulders as she keyed up a new page on Reuters.

'Any positive take-up at all?'

'A very real maybe, Declan. First Boston, one of the best. Provided the right news comes in from

Germany – ' And as she spoke the Reuters screen unscrolled its secret:

> Results in German Regional Elections
> give the Social Democrats a controlling
> position in the Bundestag this autumn.
> Of immediate significance to the Treasury
> market is their intention to impose
> withholding tax on German notes . . .

Sirkka screamed and Declan kissed her cheek, pointing to the screen above the Reuters: already the Deutschmark showed a half point increase. The phone at her elbow jumped.

'Hi.' Sirkka was at Mach 3. 'I want to trade the whole position. They're worth a point over Friday's price. Are you in? Great. I'll send you a confirm now.'

The New York squawk box was suddenly a Christmas toy. 'Harry, Harry are you there?'

Harry's beery voice trumpeted back: 'Yeh, doll, don't I live here, three hundred sixty-five days a year? The genie of the box!'

'I've swung it. I got those Italy Deutschmarks back in play.

There was a momentary tinny silence. 'Oh dear, I was about to call you. I moved them – '

'What! I just placed them here in London – '

'I sold them for you, cupcake. You were in a jam and going nowhere, so I bailed you out.'

'But I'm on the point of confirming a sale – '

'Gone, girl, sold and gone and finished.'

'To who?'

'Aristotle. He called me direct. Said he'd had a bit of trouble with you so he wasn't about to risk life and limb dealing with you again. He liked what he heard about the German shift over the weekend so he reviewed his position.' Harry stalled. 'I thought I was doing you a big favour, kiddo – '

It was too late, of course. First Boston had made their purchase bid and been accepted. Sirkka was asking for serious trouble by back-stepping; it would be unethical, fatal. She switched off the New York box and faced Declan.

'You have no choice,' Declan said sadly. 'You have to go to Ari on your knees and buy back your position.'

'But the goddam price! He'll screw me into oblivion.'

'Push First Boston, you may come out square.'

Sirkka threw her head in her hands and gave a sobbing laugh. 'I can't believe it. All the worry, all the hope – and I'm back on my knees to this slimeball.'

'That's the City,' Declan said and he took the phone and dialled Ari and handed it to her.

ELEVEN

Pension
Fund

Driving past the Aldwych at nine fifty Ansen tapped the glass partition and told the driver to step on it. They were in the bank's executive Rolls, driven by the peerless Felix, an old timer who always made it to the church on time. Felix grunted annoyance and briefly tilted the accelerator. 'We can't afford to miss-hit this time,' Ansen told Declan. 'PPF are one of the juiciest numbers in town and everyone knows it. Trouble is, they're hard men. From bottom to top. Men who know life in the gutters and the heights. So they don't respond to flannel and tokens. They want to deal hard and squeeze the best positions.'

'Doesn't upset me. It's always good to know what expectations are.' Declan lied through his teeth. In fact, he was feeling wound-up and queasy, troubled that Leonard Ansen himself was tense, that the prospect was a towering one. He thought twice about over-confidence and decided to qualify: 'I just hope I'm the fellow for the job?'

Ansen gave his first smile of the day. 'You've got a brain. Just keep on driving it.'

The Pacific Pension Fund building in Victoria had all the elegance of a coal mine. The brick was smoke-scarred and crumbling, the doorman first cousin to a miner. Declan and Ansen rode the rope-and-gravity lift in silence, Declan flexing his damp palms, drying them along the seam of his trousers.

They were shown into a long brown room with dull brown drapes and a table carved with half a century's memo notes. The mismatched chairs were comically askew and littered with yesterday's newspapers, trade magazines and, ironically, a paperback copy of *Khrush-chev Remembers*. Declan flicked at the book. 'Makes you feel we've drifted eastwards, doesn't it?'

Ansen remained unamused. 'Politics are a luxury for people in our business. Remember that.'

Mason entered, clad approximately in the clothes he had worn for golfing. He pressed a bell stud on the wall and immediately Ted Trelaunay, a lean, canny-faced man, materialized. After the briefest introductions the men positioned themselves at top and tail of the table and shuffled their grey notes. Ansen signalled to Declan, who sat squarely across from him.

'So this is your best?' Mason nodded to Declan.

'He's one of our senior traders. Last month he handled a major German government arbitrage – '

'We know about it,' Trelaunay said in his slow, low unfixable country accent. 'We know about Mr McConnochie.'

'Your homework is admirable,' Declan said lamely.

Mason and Trelaunay set their gaze on Declan and Mason spoke directly at him: 'You will be aware that we are over-weighted with Dutch State loans. These are producing a safe but uninspiring return. Furthermore, we understand the outlook for the Dutch economy after the next twelve months could be rocky. The bottom line is, we want to shift out of guilders into a position that's more . . . let's say vibrant.'

'The thing is,' Trelaunay jumped in, 'we don't intend to catch a cold like we did with you people last year. That junk market deal devalued our bonds by thirty per cent – '

'May I ask . . . ?' Declan cut in. 'Simple question. Since our people let you down, and I know we did, why come back to the table with us?'

Mason grinned to Trelaunay, who grinned to Ansen. 'This boy has a head on him. Logic appeals. I like that. All right, sonny, I'll say it straight. Shane Longman walks the line. Anyone who studies the markets knows that Shane is the best yet for big returns. It's wild and risky, but mostly it yields. Does that answer your question?'

'PPF likes to play in the big game?'

'We're here to put money in the bank, yes.' His eyes roved. 'Despite appearances.'

Trelaunay was quick to add the threat: 'That said, we do not look for unnecessary risks. When we embark on something – especially something as big as this – we *must* be sure of it. And of our partners.'

'If I personally can reassure you in any way – ?'

'What is your interpretation of the guilders market?'

'Traditionally solid, but one which gives a lower yield . . .' Declan knew this was acid-test time. 'I'm a little worried about inflation, and the knock-on effect on interest rates. Looks to me like a fifty basis points hike – '

'Over what period of time?' Trelaunay clung.

'The market has started to feel shaky. A currency realignment appears to be imminent . . .' He saw Trelaunay's attention waver and decided it was time to pounce: 'You might want to look at the French franc. The French economy is relatively strong. Levels between US, Germany and the UK markets have always been sound.' Now was the kill: 'I feel confident in advocating that PPF gets out of guilders and into French government paper. We can use the Futures Market for the initial swap – '

'Hold your horses, boyo.' Denzil Mason found the stub of a cigar and lit it. He blew blue smoke in Declan's direction. 'We are talking about an investment of three hundred million here. We have a responsibility to our members to advance with great caution – '

'And I am advancing with caution, sir. Once the general suggestion of your intention to move became clear to me – from what Mr Ansen indicated – I gave it profound thought.' He drew up his most sincere face: 'It's all that's occupied my mind over this weekend.'

Trelaunay started to whistle 'Colonel Bogey', low and out of key. Mason drummed his fingers, watched Trelaunay. Trelaunay turned back to Ansen. 'One billion ten year notes, Mr Ansen?'

'Shane Longman – and Declan here – can handle it, Mr Trelaunay. We are privileged to be asked, and excited by the potential.'

Trelaunay gestured to Mason to join him at the window. There in fast urgent whispers the men debated, and decided. They returned to the table.

'French francs sound interesting to us,' Mason told Declan. 'And you appear capable. Do the deal.'

Fifteen minutes after the arrival Declan and Ansen were climbing back into the Rolls. Ansen was pinch-faced in triumph. He slapped Declan's thigh. 'You did it, fella. A straight-from-the-shoulder knockout. It was the language they wanted to hear. Not too ambitious, not crazy – but not hyper-cautious either. They were obviously thinking francs, or near enough.

'That's what I guessed.'

'Can we deliver sensibly?'

'We're sitting on a pile of dead French stuff, on Jimmy Destry's book. Otherwise the market is sublimely set, it couldn't be better, I tell you.'

'Let me buy you lunch.'

'It's too early for lunch.'

'Can you stomach a glass of champagne at this hour?'

Declan made a mysterious face. 'Normally I wouldn't but . . . shall I tell you a secret I share with Greta Garbo? Both of us detest birthdays. Today, regretfully, is mine.'

'Well then! It can only be champagne!'

'You flung your dad out of the house?' Jimmy gasped, examining Chas's face in the next door mirror in disbelief. Ted, the men's room attendant, pricked up his ears and directed a vicious disapproving stare across at them.

'And Mother. I had to, Jimmy. It was eight o'clock. Louise was making me breakfast. We were running late after last night's bash. The doorbell went, and there they were, bags and all. I had to make an on-the-spot decision. Let them in and go through it all again, or stand my ground and say, no way. I did give them a chance. They got into the hall and then mother made a not-nice remark to Louise, implying she was some kind of whore, and I said, that's it. Get out.'

'Wow! Did they object?'

'Did they ever!' Chas pulled down his lower lip. Something came into focus for me when it all got rough.

I suddenly said to myself: this isn't loving concern, this isn't what a caring family should be about. A lot of things flashed through my head: Louise, and the way her family situation ended up – everything. Did I ever tell you her trouble?' Jimmy shrugged. 'Without going into details, let's just say there was a little overstepping of privilege by a stepfather. That's what made her run away – '

'Christ, Chas, why didn't you tell me? If I'd known – '

'She doesn't want anyone to know. She wants to drop it. It's the past, it's behind her, she just wants to get on with her adult life.' He paused, reflected. 'You know, having her around has been good for us all. She's tidied us up – '

'Forced us to buy furniture.'

'That too,' Chas laughed. 'But most of all she's focussed me. I don't think I would have been able to handle my folks the way I did today if it wasn't for Louise. I'm grateful to her for that. Deeply grateful.'

Jimmy mimed the gypsy violinist. 'Hark, do we hear the sound of heavenly choirs?'

'Don't go all funny on me!'

'Seriously, Chas – is it romance?'

'Me? Hell, Jimmy, I'm only a kid. You're the guy with the bedside locker full of little black books, all of 'em crammed to bustin'. You're the boogie boy. What about your romantic progress?'

Jimmy dropped the game and spoke from the heart. 'You know what bothers me, Chas? I can't seem to find a real woman. Someone who gives a damn whether I wash behind my ears or not. What is it about James Xavier Destry? I'm presentable. I'm generous. I earn good dough. But no woman worth anything is the slightest bit interested. No one calls me up and says, "Hi, I'm Miss X and I'd like to – " '

The door of the men's room opened and Hudson looked in: 'Jimmy, a call for you. A woman. Stephanie Keys.'

'Stephanie Keys?' Chas echoed.

Chas and Jimmy exchanged a piercing look. '*The* Stephanie Keys?' Jimmy swooned. 'No, that's just not feasible. The same Stephanie Keys who wiped my nose and slapped my bum – '

'You'd be so lucky!'

' – and sent me running for cover? It can't be She-who-must-be-obeyed.'

'It's what the man said.'

'What can she want with a minnow like me?'

'Go and find out.'

This was history-making. Jimmy danced to his station proudly and took the line. His day was all of a sudden shining down on him.

'Stephanie! I'm flattered that you remember me. The last time we spoke was so brief – '

'Jimmy. I got to thinking we were a little formal last time.'

'I'm a guy who likes to get to know – ' Jimmy relaxed too quickly but was suddenly knocked sideways.

'Meet me for lunch.'

'Well . . . yes . . . I would like – '

'Today. Samson's. One. Tell Alfredo you're with me.' And the line went dead.

In a dream Jimmy drifted back to Chas's desk, moving like a wraith past Wendy and Sirkka whose side-of-mouth questions he ignored. 'She wants me,' he told Chas.

'For what?'

'Lunch. Now.'

'There's got to be some mistake.'

But was Chas joking?

Jimmy kept a grip on his pride, changed his shirt in the men's room and slapped on some sexy Dali balm. His work concentration was gone so, rather than idle at a screen, he left the building and started out across town towards Samson's. All the way he tried to figure Stephanie Keys's angle, but every step brought more confusion. If she wanted an earnest swap she'd target higher, most likely dealing with Leonard Ansen. Any grade of deal below that would still merit a call to Wendy, or Sirkka even – but hardly him. In no conceivable circumstances would she deal – directly – with him.

In Samson's at one there was no sign of her and Jimmy found Alfredo, the rolly-polly boss, and delivered his message. Alfredo rose graciously to the hint of Stephanie and positioned Jimmy under the huge stained-glass window, in the best seat in the restaurant. A complimentary drink was served and Jimmy waited, shredding a matchstick.

At one twenty Stephanie swept in, overwhelming him in a blast of Giorgio and glittering teeth and playful eyes. She wore a brocaded Zandra Rhodes dress, more evening than day-wear, with a brooch of opal that reluctantly held the two halves of cloth across her thrusting bust. She dominated effortlessly, commanding the waiters – the restaurant – with clicking fingers and dazzling glances. Menus were perused, wines discussed, menus rewritten. She ordered for both of them, insisting on wholesome vegetarian.

'I'm very flattered that after last time you should ask me – ' Jimmy began, but she overrode him.

'I know my friends,' she said. 'This is a jungle, you agree?' It was a demand; 'So one is always out-foxing the opposition.' She detected a sudden wariness in him and softened her tack. 'What I mean is, I constantly

look out for talent I might wish to employ at competitive
rates.'

'Are you offering me a job?'

'No. But I might. What are you paid at Shane?'

'Fifty. With bonuses I can do sixty, sixty-three – '

'It's nothing.'

'I agree. For someone with my potential – '

He withered under her stare. She was smiling at him,
a lop-sided pursed-lipped smile that might be mocking,
or might be angry. He was attracted to her, but wanted
to be away, to be safely in hiding under some table
somewhere.

'Tell me about some of your good deals?'

Steady on here, Jimmy told himself. You're out of
your depth and she's a shark with an appetite. Go for
shore. Quick. He hid his unease behind a cigarette. 'It's
a matter of policy not to talk about clients and deals,'
he said with all the confidence he could drum up.

She smiled again, with sunshine. 'I like you, Jimmy.
You're young but you're not naïve. You're like me.
You tell it straight.' She winked. 'Next week we'll have
dinner. In my place.' She winked again.

'I would look forward to that.'

'So – without breaking any company secrets – what
are you working on at present?'

'French francs. I'm doing real well – '

'Funny, that's not what I heard. I heard Leonard
Ansen pulled you off certain positions and gave the
book to Declan McConnochie.'

'That's something else entirely. It's of no conse-
quence. Ansen's trying to woo a major pension fund,
Declan's been a bit doddery so . . .' He held himself.
This was too much.

'I also hear you're long in the franc.'

Jimmy frowned. 'Tell me, if you hear so many bad rumours, why am I of interest to you?'

'You are daring. I hear that too.'

He smiled, gratified. Yes, he was daring. Too daring even for Shane, he sometimes thought.

'I could be a buyer for your francs.'

Jimmy soared. It was true: his francs position was a mess, had been for a month. He was long, with no sign of a change in climate, and he was beginning to panic.

'What do you need?'

'Eight to ten year notes, Jimmy. Half a billion US equivalent. Is that too heady for you?'

'Maybe, maybe not.' He shrugged and chanced a hard-trade look. 'What's in it for me?'

She laughed mildly. 'Do you need to ask that after all we've said?'

He laughed too. 'I don't want you to think I'm a push-over, that's all.'

'Come on, Jimmy. We are both adults. I'll help you unload a dead position at a good mid-market price. It suits me and it suits you. Plus I want to see you dealing a bit, I want to see your style.' Her eyes became moody and suggestive. 'I want to see some more of you. Now, does that all make sense or does it not?'

He reached across the table and dared: he held her hand. 'Yes, we're adults,' he said.

In a world of computers where money was a science, Leonard Ansen preferred pen and paper and the answers of his instincts. Now, mid-afternoon on the first day of this pioneering week, he sat, pen poised above a virgin scribble pad, with Peter Longman at the end of a telephone line, trying to focus cavalier chit-chat but all the time figuring a strategy for Shane's future. As Longman rambled on about falling hotel standards and his upcoming travels, Ansen wrote the words: *Control Wolf. Win the Public. New growth stage.*

Peter Longman seemed to divine his thoughts and scribbles. 'You need an idea,' Longman said suddenly, incisively. 'And I'm not sure you'll find it in the money market. You need to redesign Shane and change the emphasis. I am confident in your team, Leonard. But I am not confident in the bank's future as long as these haggling wars go on. The executive upsets will ultimately ruin us all. It filters down. The traders become polluted, the prospective buyers become suspicious . . .' He sighed in frustration. 'Am I making sense, or am I too old and too one-track-minded?'

'You're right on the button, Peter. Shane is poised like it never has been. We are going one of two ways: fast up, or fast down. I believe, as you believe, that it's all a question of investors' confidence. As you're speaking I'm taking notes about a strategy for change. Immediately on my agenda – like today – is a meeting with my best people: Hudson, Wendy, Max. Then I'd like your help with a plan – '

'I'm sorry, Leonard. I have to step out of the executive row situation. You must know that. I've done my bit and you have a healthy stay of execution, if that's the phrase. But I cannot be seen to be constantly upstaging internal decisions. What I'm saying is: the next move has got to be yours and you have got to push it through by tact and persuasion.'

'I understand perfectly.' Ansen chuckled. 'Any ideas yourself?'

'Sure. Push Lee Wolf out of a window. A high one.'

'Give me a few days. Take consolation from the fact that the team is wound up nicely. Declan is now on the brink of the best thing he's ever done.'

'I'm encouraged. Just let's break that executive stale-mate once and for all. Let's find the new Shane, Leonard. Let's move on.'

When Longman rang off Ansen summoned his 'best people'. In ten minutes they sat before him, pads in hand, eager for battle. Ansen repeated Longman's concerns and specified the need for a plan to redefine the bank.

'Mergers, take-overs, grand-scale operations – that's the future,' Hudson opined. 'Maybe Wolf is partly right in that the departments at Shane need to be realigned?'

'No,' Wendy said. 'We are not grand-scale. Not yet. We are a middle-size bank with a recent tradition of good gambling. The big danger is over-ambition. Yes, I support Leonard in his desire for fringe risk-taking. And yes, I know we are grievously handicapped by executive dissent. But I think the answer must be subtler – '

'Win the public,' Max said suddenly.

Ansen looked twice at him, then down at the note he had notched on his pad. 'Tell me more, Max?'

'Seems to me the bank lacks the lure of an image. We still retain that olde-worlde sense of a Longmans long departed. That establishes the gravity that makes Lee Wolf and the others pull away from new ideas, new risks. And they can argue, as they do, that they are delivering what the clients expect. Shane Longman clients expect a grey, traditional old service, the style that was established so many years ago.'

'You're saying we should plan an advertising campaign?'

'Maybe not.' Max's voice intoned upwards and he tapped the side of his nose. The Alchemist mask drew over his face. 'Advertising per se may not be enough.

What I want to say to our clients is: we are different. We have courage. Yes or no?'

'You are stealing my phrase,' Wendy said.

'Then our campaign must show courage.'

'I know you, Max,' Ansen said. 'You have something in mind.'

'Yes I do. It's a tremendous and lucky coincidence. I need to make a call.' He got to his feet. 'Can we all be here later – say, seven this evening? I'd like you to meet someone.'

Everyone agreed to a seven o'clock resumption and he meeting split as a call came down from James Farrell, seeking Ansen.

Ansen rode the lift to the executive floor and joined Farrell taking coffee by the window which gave the building's best street vista.

'The DTI situation is formally settled and I've given some trade interviews today damning their procedure,' Farrell said. 'Furthermore, I've memo'd the group that the New Profile proposal has been indefinitely postponed. The books look good all of a sudden, so your team is relatively secure. However – ' he pushed a coffee over to Ansen and Ansen saw that it, compared to Farrell's cup, was rich and strong '– I'm obliged to caution you. The events of the last week write it in bold letters. You have Longman on your side, and you have me. Longman cannot go on interfering and as for me . . .' He sighed tiredly. 'I won't last forever, Leonard. I might not even hold the pace a year. I want to give you notice of that.'

'I appreciate your honesty with me, James.'

'I want you to win.' Farrell was gearing forward and speaking with a straining passion. 'I want you to be the one to carry the Longman flag and make this bank grow into something we can all be proud of. But Lee is tough and his support is no weaker. There are those who will resent what Peter Longman did and you must be ready for them. Don't allow anything to taint you again. Lee plays dead straight, that's his supreme advantage – '

'*No one* plays dead straight, James.'

James Farrell stopped and finished his coffee. His interrogative gaze was softened by a grin. 'I should know you better. You are calm and smiling. You know something that I don't know. Care to share it?'

'Need to know: the MI6 policy. Let's acknowledge the wisdom in that. No matter what anyone says, I am squeaky clean. So, I'm certain, are you. I won't taint you with what I know because you don't need to involve yourself.' He leaned across and patted Farrell's arm. 'I want you to do me a favour, James. Over and above all this in-fighting is . . . life. I want you to look after Number One, get your health together and forget everything else.'

'I'll repeat it, Leonard. After me, I want it to be you. Don't let me down.'

'I'll do my best.'

Fortified by Farrell's commitment Ansen drifted down through the trading floor and spot-checked the stations. Everything was barrelling impressively, with a special buzz around Chas as he shifted half a million's worth of bonds.

Sirkka, on the other hand, was riding a low tide, angrily brawling with Hannah over a systems query. 'All I'm saying is the system must be leaking,' Sirkka demanded.

Hannah was equally vociferous: 'And all I'm saying is a systems set-up cannot leak. You don't understand the technology, Sirkka, so don't jump to conclusions.'

'Then someone's cracked into it and stolen my thunder. Someone's passing out my information. Look, I typed it up here. Read it. Compare what Forex are pushing. Compare what Markstein is pushing – '

Declan hurried up in a flap. 'You shut me off, Hannah – '

'I'm sorry. I was trying to demonstrate to Sirkka that her system was sound – '

'Well I'm up to my eyes working out projections. I need my screens, so lay off, will you?'

'Are you making progress?' Ansen asked.

Declan shrugged and chewed his well-chewed pencil. 'We're sitting on those in-house francs, which is terrific. Right now I'm more concerned about getting rid of the guilders – '

'I've got a guilders buyer.'

Everyone turned. Michelle romped up brightly, thrilled with her coup. She addressed herself exclusively, warmly, to Declan: 'Melina Lau at the Tokyo Pension Fund, an old pal. She's looking for a long term – '

Declan couldn't resist it. He grabbed her in front of the audience and hugged her hard. She recoiled, took a step back and looked at him through narrowed, fresh eyes. Declan's mind raced, he blushed madly. 'Guilders are good,' he started to stammer. 'Hudson says so . . . the Dutch economy is in a flat spot but Hudson says it will be over inside twenty-four months – '

'You don't have to sell it to us, Declan,' Ansen smiled, observing the arc of electricity sparking. 'Just go and net a big institutional client and let's put PPF to bed.' He semaphored quietly to Sirkka and Hannah who discreetly turned back to the flickering terminal. 'Night or day, Declan, get on to me as soon as the deal is in place. That's a special moment I want to share.'

'You got it.'

Declan moved away beside Michelle. She was sheepish and unusually shy of him. For his part, he was more edgy than ever. The feel of her lingered, it was juvenile stuff, the stuff of teen dreams. But what was she thinking?

'I appreciate your isolating that number for me,' he said. 'Tokyo Pension are conservative, they sound ideal – '

'I think you'll have to win over Melinda first.'

They stopped by the kitchen and she said she wanted tea. They went inside and he tensed when she closed the door. He fumbled at the machine, making her tea and scalding himself at the same time. He handed her the cup – the only decent china cup in the place – and looked at her over the rim.

'You know,' she said. 'I hate those movies where the pilot faces the girl before the big battle and she says to him, do it for me. Win it for me.' She shied away again, then came back to his eyes. 'But I'm saying it anyway. I know how big this is and I want you to do us all proud. Win it, Declan.'

TWELVE

Corrida
with Wolf

They were sitting in Ansen's office – Wendy, Hudson and Ansen himself – when a vision from Pamplona, from a Spanish bullring on a summer's afternoon, stepped in. Max tagged after this spangled heroic figure who wore his jet black hair, like Max's, in a swept-slick, but much longer, ponytail. Wendy felt her jaw droop and snapped it shut, Hudson sounded an audible 'Huh?' and Ansen settled his chin patiently in his hands.

The man wore a black baggy linen jacket over his sequined shirt and apron-fronted trousers and carried impressive rolls of fine art paper under his arm. His grin silenced all questions. It flooded the room gloriously, a grin from ear to ear that made a handsome face gorgeous. Wendy felt the attraction that all women who met Gabriel Romero Mara felt, a brutal attraction, fully physical, that almost embarrassed her. Here was a gypsy, a Barbary pirate, Valentino reborn.

'Mr Mara is a good friend of mine,' Max began proudly. 'That is to say, we met at the dentist's the other day. But I knew of him. *Everybody* knows of him. Everybody knows he is better than Christo.'

Wendy frowned, thinking, *Christo who? Should* I know him? Is he from Hollywood? Max has flipped. He wants some B-picture actor to elevate the company's PR!

'I shall allow Mr . . . eh, Señor . . . Mara to speak for himself. Gabriel?'

The Spaniard chose a careful spot dead centre of the carpet in front of Ansen's desk. He put aside his art rolls and took the two newspapers Max had been carrying, a *Financial Times* and a copy of the *Sun*. He didn't speak. He bowed from the waist, deeply, then started to separate the pages of the newspapers and crunch them into loose balls. When he had finished all the pages he reached into his pocket, withdrew a clear plastic sheet and spread it conscientiously on the carpet. Ansen hid a smile behind his hands. The effect was that of watching a cabaret magician, or an inspired clown at a French circus. It was amusing, but it was also – thanks to the Spaniard's grace of movement and appearance – hypnotic.

When the clear sheet was in place Mara went on hands and knees and placed the rolled newspaper pages one on top of the other in a rough pyramid. Then he reached back into his baggy coat, extracted a paint-spray can and started to spray the newspapers red. After a minute he pocketed the red paint and withdrew a black paint-spray can. With a flourish he finished the spray job, blurring the glittering postbox red with dashes of lustrous black. In an acrobatic backward jolt he found his feet, spread his arms and addressed Ansen: '*Voila!* Ze Face of a Nation!'

'Art,' was all Ansen could think of saying.

'Art is a limitation. Ze Word. I call it *Aaa!* Ze initiator of all sings. Ze beginning.'

Ansen looked at Wendy, who appeared sincerely entranced. Admiring? Or just bemused by Max's proposition? Hudson sat gaga.

'You are an artist?'

'Ze artist of ze environment. I cannot describe, so I do. I am not afraid of ze Christo whom zey say is ze best in ze world. I cannot see what he sees. Instead I see ze little sings. Ze whispers and ze jokes – like zis – ' He swept an arm affectionately towards the soggy newspapers. 'Or I see ze big sings. Ze – how you say it?'

Max obliged. 'Statements.'

'Ay, ze statements. Statements zat one makes which affect ze process of life which is evolution.'

Wendy looked warily into Ansen's face, then boldly to Max. 'If you could clarify for us, Max – ?'

'Don't you see? Gabriel is one of the finest emerging environmental artists. Look!' In a burst of enthusiastic energy Max unrolled Mara's artwork, huge sketched impressions – and some photographs – of outrageous 'outdoor' artworks. One sketch showed a Venetian waterway bedecked with balloons. Another picture showed the Hall of Prayer in Peking, silk-wrapped. Another, a photo, showed a New York building wrapped in what looked suspiciously like toilet paper. 'And here, cuttings from *Newsweek*, from *Paris Match . . .*'

'Isn't that the Standard Life building on Madison?'

'Yes,' Mara bragged. 'I call it Money Is Paper.'

Ansen was tempted to laugh aloud in appreciation of this evident wit, but thought better of it. Both Max and Mara took the business very seriously.

'How does this fit in with our schemes?' Hudson said bluntly.

'Gentlemen, Wendy, you are looking at a genius. People speak of him as they spoke of the young Picasso, Henry Moore, Rodin. Already he has raised more than a million dollars in various sponsorships. All have been controversial. Standard is the biggest. No one else – no corporate bod – has taken the chance.' Max swung into the chair in front of Ansen and pleaded: 'Gabriel has a project he wishes to fulfil. A daring project that celebrates 1992 and the twenty-first century. A project that is significantly and historically British, but speaks to the future. He needs a hundred thousand pounds to realize it. I am proposing that we at Shane invest in Gabriel and his project. It becomes *our* statement for 1992 and the twenty-first century.'

'What's the project, Max?'

'Gabriel?' Max side-stepped.

Mara came forward dutifully to address Ansen with a garlic-flavoured passion to match Max's: 'Ze project is to wrap up ze White Cliffs of Dover in parachute silk.'

Ansen couldn't help it: he laughed out loud. Wendy split a grin. Even Hud twitched.

'Absurd!'

'But ingenious, Leonard.' Max banged the desk. 'Can you see it? Dover. Landbridge Europe. And the slogan will be: "Shane Longman Wraps up the Future".'

Everyone suddenly paused for a rethink. Mara was smiling again, victoriously. Max, by his side, smiled along. Ansen moved a pen over his desk pad, no longer laughing. 'How will this hundred grand be dispersed?'

'Salaries, materials, a video link system that's essential in so vast a project. I mean, it will take a crew of thirty people to assemble it. It will take a fortnight to actually wrap the cliffs. He'll need two helicopters for most of that time – '

'Crazy – ' Hudson muttered under his breath, but without conviction.

Ansen spoke over him: 'Standard paid to have this job done on their building?'

'Absolutely, Leonard. And you've no idea what attention it brought them. A media deluge lasting weeks. Plus it was reckoned that the passer-by, the average man, made a more vivid connection between the sponsor and the piece. I spoke with the ad agency that looks after Standard. They said it was their most productive venture. Their only complaint was that its way-outness opposed their previous high-density campaigns to some extent and one contradicted and weakened the other. In Shane's case that problem is not applicable. We avoid institutional advertising. We work on organic tradition.' He banged the desk again. 'But now we are looking for a break from tradition. You and Longman and all of us want something brand *new*. Something that speaks of our courage, and our ambition.'

There were no objections round the desk now. Hudson took up the rolls of artwork and reviewed them earnestly, whispering to a serious-faced Wendy.

'I'll need to take it upstairs,' Ansen said. 'That means tackling James Farrell . . . and Lee Wolf. Plus all points between.'

'But you like the notion?'

Ansen took the Standard picture and smiled again, genuinely tickled. 'It sure beats chucking money behind some boring old opera.'

Mara thumped his golden chest and boomed, 'Leave it to me. I will make you all famous!'

Wendy imagined Lee Wolf's response to toilet rolls

and *Sun* sculptures and she smiled back at Mara with a fading optimism.

'What do you mean the system could be infiltrated?'

'Technically it's possible, that's what I'm saying. Don't you start shouting at me too!'

'I'm sorry, Hannah. I never was good at all this computer-speak. It sounds mildly obscene to me. I'm for the traditional days of J. Paul Getty and a sharp pencil . . .' Ansen flicked the pages of the scribbled report that Hannah had prepared about the 'leak' affecting the Shane system. 'In common English you're saying our Eyes Only material could be tapped?'

'That would be a complex and extravagant piece of industrial espionage. But any system could be cracked, given the code.'

'Which is what you suspect?'

'The system's sound. But there's a hint of leakage. These things happen. Intentionally, or by fluke. As I outline in that report we're working flat out to investigate it. But I thought it proper to advise you of all possibilities.'

'Thank you for alerting me. Keep at it.'

Wendy came up, fresh from her morning's meditation, bright as a lark. 'I know about the gremlins,' she said, 'but they're not going to get me down today. I feel ready for anything. Last night I dreamed of Gabriel Mara. I was in the gallery while he fought a raging corrida. The bull was Wolf. Anyway, he slayed the bull and threw the ear to me. I ate it.'

'Weren't you ill? He's poisonous, you know.'

They walked down the bustling aisles, each thrilling to the busy bank sounds. Sirkka waved to them and they were cheered to see her relatively clear-eyed and calm. 'I asked for the executive meeting to discuss the bank promotion,' Ansen said, 'but Wolf obstructed. Max tells me that Mara's the kind of fellow who won't wait around. He has the offer of an environmental piece in Hong Kong and he'll take it up unless he gets his sponsorship here – '

'How long will he wait?'

'Just today. He wants confirmation today.'

'And Wolf?'

'He says he'll let me know. He's busy on a Mickey Mouse acquisition.'

'Run the vote without him.'

'Don't think I didn't think of it. But he's the one really responsible for the corporate image.'

'Pressurize him.'

'Don't worry. I'm committed to Max's idea. It's another of those hare brained schemes that sounds too bad to be true until you really examine it.' He narrowed his eyes towards her. 'And now you're going to assume the Wary Wendy role and tell me I'm insane and should be locked away with Max – ?'

'Not at all. This time I'm yours – '

'Oh? Mara sweep your affections so easily?' There was a tinge, the faintest tinge, of jealousy in his words.

'Yes, he *is* handsome. But of course it's more than that. Maybe I'm growing up. Delayed action, most likely. All of a sudden I think twice about things. So I don't judge Max so quickly. Yes, I think a lot of his ideas are lamentable. But I also know he is a genius himself. I respect his opinions. And I respect yours. I saw how you were taken by Mara and the whole notion. I saw the dawning in your face – '

'I spoke with Peter Longman last night. Filled him in. He didn't even laugh. He knows this Christo. Says Mara is a wizard protégé. Peter plays up to his Philistine side, but in fact he's an active follower of the arts. He thought the idea was a winner.'

'But he's not involving himself?'

'It doesn't concern him. It's over to me now – and the board.'

Declan stood up from his station and bumped into Wendy as she rounded the corner with Ansen. He looked scrubbed, laundered and excited and his brief-case shone importantly in his hand.

'The guilders?' Ansen asked.

'On my way to unload,' Declan said. 'I hope. Any last advice?'

'Yes,' Wendy said. 'Treat a woman like a man and a man like a woman. That's great advice for tiring Lotharios.'

'You must mean my brother, the rake?' Declan joked. 'I'm a trader, pure and simple.'

'Good luck,' Ansen said, and was touched when Declan shook his hand.

All the way across London Declan was reciting parrot-style the speech he would make. He coached himself aggressively: this was just another pitch, only different from the others in its monumental size. But that was not entirely true. This was a different type of pitch, from a different type of Declan McConnochie. Ansen and Wendy were taking a big chance on this one. This one mattered, really mattered, and they set it squarely and solely on *his* shoulders. They trusted him at a time when he needed people to re-evaluate and trust him and he would not, could not, let them down.

Melinda Lau had asked that they meet in the leafy surroundings of Lincoln's Inn fields. A strikingly tall Japanese woman of about thirty-five beckoned to him from across the park. The punctuality of the meeting impressed: she had requested it for twelve and it was now, to the second, twelve midday.

She sat with him on a bench. 'Do you know the expression *Herkos odonton*, Mr McConnochie?' She asked the question in the comfortable certitude that he did not.

'Yes,' Declan said. 'It's from classical Greek. It means, "behind the hedge of the teeth". In other words, top secret.'

Her eyes flashed wide for a second. 'You are educated.'

'Incompletely and unsuccessfully. But it is flattering to meet someone who can acknowledge at least my effort. I'm a street kid who worked hard and won scholarships and constantly failed examinations. I wanted a career in law, but everyone took it so seriously and I was, I'm afraid, not so serious. I have made many errors of judgement in my life, and many errors of, shall we say, effort. But sometimes . . .'

She gave him a surprising smile. A smile from the heart. 'You talk a lot.'

'I'm sorry. It's the way we've come to meet. My very good friend Michelle Hauptmann made the indirect introduction. I value her very highly and I'm inclined to look on her friends as my friends.'

'You and she are . . . lovers?'

Declan smiled back. The question was out of order and both of them knew it. He need not answer, should not answer, the intimacy was a trap. 'No,' he said. 'We are not lovers.'

'And you are not married?'

'No.'

'Why did I think that?'

This was a game Declan had once excelled at. This

woman was a willing participant – and gentle, pleasant and lovely to boot. In different circumstances . . . He shrugged away his own imaginings. Truth was, he wasn't much interested.

'I have a guilders position I want to move quickly,' he said. 'The details are here – ' He handed her a paper. 'Michelle felt you might be open to such a purchase.'

'*Herkos odonton,*' she grinned. 'We are looking for a new long term position – ' She slipped on spectacles and glanced at Declan's proposal. 'And yes, the numbers look big enough.' She twitched the glasses to peer across the frame: 'Is there anything insidious about your urgency and directness?'

Declan spread his hands innocently. 'Not in the slightest. Our client has seen another market that he's interested in. He needs the liquidity as soon as possible. I have nothing to hide – '

'Except your feelings?' She sent an impish sneer. 'This is a big purchase,' she resumed. 'Maybe we could have dinner tonight and discuss its ramifications? I'd very much like to hear your long view on the market.'

'But you have your own long view,' Declan said sweetly. 'Dinner wouldn't alter that.'

She considered his face closely, then lowered her head and barked a laugh. 'I should be very offended. The fascination of Western men for Eastern women never fails me. I have yet to pass a transaction of this size without an evening tryst.'

'Let this be the first time.' He paused. 'And, by the way, I find you very sensitive and very lovely.'

She laughed again, then stood. A new persona emerged, an iron butterfly from a sugary chrysalis. 'Very well, Mr McConnochie, I will review your position and consider it against our requirement. Your presentation is good and that will speed up our decision process. So rest assured we will let you know shortly.'

'Not now?'

'No, not now.'

Declan contained his disappointment. He closed his case and moved away. He turned to thank her, with grace and aplomb, and she looked at him – piercingly – and smiled.

Mabel, Wolf's secretary, called down to Ansen's office, late and inconvenient, with the instruction that Lee Wolf was now available to talk. Ansen was hectically busy closing a tactical bond management deal, but Mara had been on the telephone three times during the afternoon and Max had been blowing hot in his ear, so he abandoned his deal.

The meeting, surprisingly, was in Wolf's panelled office, a hideous example of minimalist endeavour made tolerable only by the covered Hepplewhite desk and the oak walls. A Hockney, some windows and some valueless glittering trophies brightened the long room but did nothing to assuage Leonard Ansen's claustrophobia. Whenever he came here he felt small and young and inadequate, like he had stepped back to childhood and stumbled into the spoilt school bully's den. Wolf knew Ansen's oppression too, it seemed, and whenever he particularly wished to rub Leonard's nose in it, it was here he chose to do it.

James Farrell, Ralph Goldring and Liz Armitage, the faceless, under-utilized PR officer, were seated around Wolf's desk, and Peter Wainwright, the rarely-to-be-found in-house lawyer, perched, smoking a cheroot, on the windowsill. Ansen understood immediately: he had given away too much in his phone call preparations for the meeting. Armitage and Wainwright were in Wolf's pocket and, yes, Wolf was the man who held the purse strings. The full executive meeting had been short-circuited and this was on offer, a twisted travesty that could yield only one result.

'What about the others?' Ansen asked anyway.

Farrell squirmed in his seat. 'I, er, gave everyone a clear indication of what was proposed. Four of our people are out of the country anyway, so Lee thought – '

'I gather you have a radical PR concept?' Wolf cut in brusquely, smilingly. 'Most of all, this concerns Liz and Peter, is my reckoning.'

Ansen decided to avoid early confrontation. He shrugged and unrolled the best of Mara's artwork and began a concise and articulate lecture. As he spoke Farrell's attention warmed by the minute, but Liz and Peter Wainwright looked appalled. Lee Wolf, for his part, looked like he knew what was coming and was past surprise.

'But this sponsorship would carry the bank into the front pages,' Liz Armitage said breezily.

'That's correct. And every investor reads the front pages.'

'That's the smart answer, Leonard,' Wolf said, adding, 'respectfully.' He chewed the end of a Havana and lit up, offering the box, selectively, to Wainwright and Goldring.

'Smart is not a word that embarrasses me. We need to be smart right now, Lee. Gabriel Romero Mara is an emerging phenomenon. Far-sighted patrons will be amply rewarded in time – '

'We are not into long term promotions that cost the earth today,' Liz Armitage persisted. 'Our advertising budget, if it might immodestly be termed such, has been small and sensible – '

'And now we need to change our image.'

'That is a matter of opinion, Leonard.' Lee Wolf's eyes blazed attack. 'And you know where I stand on the matter.' He fingered one of Mara's illustrations in a dismissive, uninterested way. 'This stuff reminds me of what Warhol said: these days everyone's gonna be famous for fifteen minutes. I mean, I like it fine but – '

'I didn't know you had expertise in the field of modern art,' Ansen said. 'You favour Warhol?'

Wolf chewed his lip, spat cigar smoke. He laughed in a scolding, patient way and turned to Farrell. 'There is merit in what Leonard says about our profile. Association with successful modern art is no bad notion – ' Farrell thumbed the *Newsweek* cuttings and looked towards Peter Wainwright. Wainwright gave a pale-faced, plaintive nod towards Liz Armitage.

'Liz?'

'I cannot see the merits. I am proud of our conservative management of advertising finances – '

'Can I see you alone a moment, Lee?' Ansen was suddenly staring very hard at Wolf and in an instant Wolf sensed trouble, saw his hide on the line and softened his expression. The response encouraged Ansen immeasurably. Uneasy, Wolf slipped out from behind his desk, excused himself and led Ansen into the connecting secretary's office. Mabel was readying herself to leave and Ansen waited till she was through, biding his time, making himself comfortable in one of the leather waiting room chairs.

When at last the secretary departed Wolf sat on her desk and grinned at Ansen. He looked serene, but the edges of his eyes showed yellowish-white, pinched with tension. 'So what can I do for you?'

'I wanted to talk with you before I talked with Peter Wainwright.'

Wolf continued to be achingly amiable. 'Why do you want to talk with Peter Wainwright?'

'To find out the legal implications of something I heard. Something sad and distressing that relates to this management team.'

'I can't imagine – '

'I spoke with a man called Sean Evans. Investment Adviser for Lowenstein, you might recall him?'

Wolf's features drooped. His eyes became hounded, terrified. 'I hardly know him.'

'That's curious. Because he knows you well. Apparently you often drank together? Sean likes the booze, it appears. And one night not too long ago, when he was on the point of breaking with Lowenstein, you two had a long boozy session and he made the mistake of being indiscreet.'

'I don't know what you're talking about.'

'He recalls. Vividly. He sobered up the next day and realized what he'd told you – about the Vellor and Marks take-over – might be dangerous to him. You assured him that it would go no further. At that point, apart from the three-man board at Lowenstein, no one else knew what was cooking.'

Wolf fell silent, his cigar running cold. He kept staring, slack-jawed, at Ansen.

'Billy Lang got the tip from you, conveniently leaving out your source, or the nature of the take-over. Billy was Max's man, and Max was mine.'

'It's all perfectly legal. If I let something slip – '

'You're right, Lee. Except that would not be Sean Evans's evidence. Because somewhere during the course of your boozy evening you confided to Sean that you wanted the inside lowdown on Lowenstein to try and shake up some dirt against me.' Ansen was tempted to shout it out; instead he spoke with the steady delight of an easy win. 'You got indiscreet yourself, Lee. When Evans realized the sequence of probable events he was ready and keen to talk. He didn't want his job chances to be destroyed if another DTI inquiry started. It was a booze-up that went over the top, pure and simple. As soon as he was aware of his mistake he called you and begged you. You gave him assurances.'

'It's not a case,' Wolf said, his voice hoarse with fear.

'Maybe not. I'll ask Peter – ' Ansen started for the door.

'Just a minute.'

Lee Wolf blocked Ansen's move to the door and extended his hands, placing them on Ansen's shoulders. Ansen could smell the fear on his breath. The American's gaze – first time ever – was unsteady. He spoke:

'The word "partner" implies, for me, a kind of brother. We are brothers, but there's something wrong with the way we conduct ourselves. We share no trust, and that is wrong – '

'I don't need this, Lee. I'll lay it on straight: you played dirty and now I'll play dirty. I want that image rebuild. I want the money for Mara.'

Wolf's cowering gaze flickered with anger. 'I stated my case in front of everyone. In front of James – '

'Unstate it. Tell them we had a chat. About art and Andy Warhol. And I persuaded you to change your mind.'

'Don't push me, Leonard.'

'I think you'll find James Farrell amenable. As for the others, I wouldn't worry about them. They're expendable small fry.' He sneered. 'Wouldn't you think?'

They returned to Wolf's office in a stiff march. Liz

Armitage and Wainwright watched Wolf closely, as though they guessed a checkmate.

'I've reconsidered . . .' Wolf began, and he clumsily detailed his half-baked reasons for supporting Mara's plan, none of which was comprehensible to anyone in the office. He concluded, addressing Farrell: 'Leonard has persuaded me that it is your private hope that all of us participate in finding new ground to break, and that we establish some process of unified endeavour. Let this be the endeavour we share.'

Everyone seemed – approximately anyway – satisfied. Liz Armitage moaned on, but Wainwright, divining Wolf's distress, talked her down. 'I can't see the point,' Goldring began, but Wolf drew him aside and spoke in a hiss of emphasis, dousing all resistance.

'So,' Farrell beamed. 'We gift-wrap the Cliffs of Dover next!' He hooked Ansen's arm as they moved to exit. 'It's my birthday and Christmas rolled into one. How did you do it? Lee Wolf voting on your side! It's unthinkable.'

'Deep down I think he likes me.'

'You've made an old man very young today. Thing is, can you work that magic again?'

'I think you're about to observe the start of a new era at Shane. It's downhill from now on.'

'Never count your chickens, Leonard . . .'

THIRTEEN

Bluebirds?

The magnetic lure of Michelle was stronger than ever. Declan spent the afternoon telling himself that now was the time to be manful and disciplined but again and again he found himself running to her station to share the minor dramas of the day. His account of the exchange with Melinda Lau impressed her (he was gushing in chivalrous detail) but when he confidently asked her to join him for a drink at the Spanish Steps after work she declined, utterly deflating him.

At Sirkka's station Chas and Jimmy Destry were nudging towards fisticuffs, arguing about borrowed Treasury projections. 'You're a bloody crook,' Chas was shouting, tugging viciously at Jimmy Destry's tie. 'You don't give a damn about other people's situations . . .'

Declan was tempted to intrude. But he passed by instead, muttering towards Jimmy, 'Hey, squirt, I should have a spot for your dead francs position in the next couple of days. So keep your vim for celebrating, OK?'

Jimmy threw a muffled comment his way, then Declan took the lift to the exit and crossed towards the Spanish Steps. Entering the bistro, footfalls caught him up and an arm looped through his. Sirkka pecked his cheek, prematurely congratulating him.

'Not yet,' he said. 'It's still floating. Like my entire life, it's up in the air.'

At the bar Sirkka ordered brandy and once again Declan watched her careless appetite for alcohol and admonished her. 'Why the gloom?' she came back. 'Seems to me it's all starting to happen for you. Michelle cares. That's obvious.'

'Is it? I don't know. I worry. About my stamina. I've worked very hard for a long time and I've got nothing to show for it and I feel all of a sudden I'm back at the start.'

'I know what you mean.' She was serious and sad. She sucked at the brandy, opened her purse and took two Valium tablets. 'I'm going to Copenhagen.'

'When?'

'Day after tomorrow. For a reassessment. A to Z. My whole life. I'm going to sit down with Sven . . .' Her voice broke and she coughed to clear her throat. 'If he's still there for me. I don't know, Declan. Maybe the street is not for me. Maybe everything I told you – Africa, all that – maybe that's where I belong. James has been very kind and supportive. And Wendy.'

'We'll miss you.'

She gave a grey laugh. 'Don't. Not yet. I may be back before you know it. Sven is not a forgiving man.'

He covered her hand with his and commanded her eyes. 'You know, Sirkka, you do need Copenhagen and a break and a few days away from the treadmill. We all do. But you'd be crazy to chuck it all if your main reason is the Deutschmark fiasco.'

Sirkka's gaze drifted past him and her eyes widened fractionally. Very quickly he thought, why is she smiling? What's so amusing in all this glum self-searching? The spontaneous answer floored him. As Sirkka's grin turned to laughter a booming vocal rendition of 'Happy Birthday To You . . . !' soared behind him. He swivelled, speechless – and there was the office gang: Chas, Hannah, Max, Hudson, Jimmy, a host of senior and junior traders, the reception girls, and Wendy. Declan's eyes raced through the gang, searching her out. His heart sank. She wasn't there. She was away somewhere, motoring in the country on this fine mellow day, with Bruno most likely, reviving their promises . . . As he winged, the crowd in front of him divided and the chorus reached, 'Happy Birthday, dear Declan . . . !' The house lights went down and the yellow halo of cake lights walked out of the crowd. A large snowy cake on a silver platter, held proud by . . . Michelle.

'Well, dammit, Michelle, you could have dropped a hint!' He fell into her arms and she held him laughingly, but gripping tight.

'Happy Day, Declan.' The handshakes and hugs and smiling faces cartwheeled past, leaving him winded and smeared with ten shades of lipstick. 'Belated Happy Day!'

'Sirkka was voted to make sure you stayed here.'

'Traitor. I hate birthdays. Leonard Ansen broke the secret?'

Wendy nodded, kissed his cheek, whispered, 'Take it as a special compliment. Leonard's not a sentimental man. But he's getting mighty fond of you.'

Cake was cut, ale flowed, the singing became irreverent and serious. The little groups separated and gelled and the harmonious storm of an earnest party began. Declan moved around, politely revelling in his role as guest of honour, but then he was gravitating again towards Michelle and the nearest door.

'It really embarrasses you,' Michelle observed warmly. 'You're wriggling like a worm on a hook.'

'Some parts of growing up I'll never accept. Maybe it's something to do with my background, the way I was brought up. There never was time for affection and parties and all this – '

'But that's interesting, Declan.' She held him. 'No, really it is. You know Max once talked to me about you. The conversation was about my trip to New York, all that. Max was saying what a mystery I was. And then he said the only other mystery man in Shane was you. He couldn't figure you.' Her grip on his arm was tight, her eyes close and intense. '*I* couldn't figure you. Most of the time I saw this stupid angry cocksman. I wanted to hate him and then, every so often, the sun shone through. It baffled me. This mixture of saint and sinner. But now I'm beginning to understand a lot . . .'

Back home, all alone, the telephone rang. Declan dragged his heels to the phone, lifted it. 'Yes?'

'Mr McConnochie?' It was Melinda Lau. His knuckles tightened.

'Melinda, hi.'

'I hope I'm not disturbing you?'

'Not at all – '

'We'd like to purchase the guilder position.'

'That sounds good.'

'But we'll only go to ninety-six and an eighth. Not what you charted.'

It was perfect. He coughed to hold himself. 'Yes, I think we can work with that.'

'Excellent. I'll send you a confirm first thing in the morning.'

'Thanks, that's fine.'

'I hope your other client deal goes good.'

'So do I, thank you.'

'Oh, and Mr McConnochie? I think Michelle Hauptmann is a very fortunate lady. And that's *Herkos odonton*.'

He laughed and rang off and ran to his briefcase. He'd won it, or rather half of it. He needed to find those francs and get it set up.

But first he'd call Michelle.

He was on the racetrack again, and galloping, and there was no catching him up.

Ansen was at his desk at nine thirty when the call came through from Pacific Pension. At first he imagined it was a thank you call. Declan had rung at midnight to break the news of the Tokyo purchase and Ansen had left him gearing up for a progress call to Trelaunay first thing. But here was Denzil Mason, grim-sounding, persuasive as a blunt instrument in demanding an urgent meeting. 'I'll try to locate Declan – ' Ansen hedged, suspecting big trouble, but Mason wasn't in the mood for niceties. 'Just get him here in my office in an hour. It isn't a social call.'

On the trading floor Ansen found Declan in shirtsleeves, unbuttoned almost to the navel, raging like a mad dog in the aisles.

'What's up?'

'I'll tell you what's up! I can't find Jimmy Destry. I can't tap into his position. I can't find the francs. I know

Grenfell are sellers but I can't rouse them. I promised Trelaunay – '

'Well get ready to promise him some more. He wants us. Rather, Mason does. Now. And whatever the cause for summons, it isn't compliments.'

Side by side they moved towards the lift, just stopping to grab Declan's PPF papers and case.

In the car to Victoria, Ansen hardly spoke. Declan sat beside him rigidly, confused and steaming.

In the brown boardroom Mason and Trelaunay were waiting, equally steaming. Declan launched out in attack mode, stressing the good fortune of the Tokyo purchase, the good price, the speedy progress of the deal.

'Let's talk turkey, gentlemen.' Trelaunay was no longer interested in Declan and spoke over him: 'This morning we were offered a price on this package that beats yours by half a million dollars.'

Neither Ansen nor Declan could speak for a moment. Had PPF been price-chasing round the market? Unlikely, in view of the fact that a deal had been agreed with Shane Longman. So someone had heard about their intention – how? – and found a better way.

'Who made the offer?'

'Never you mind. I'll come to that. You assured us that Shane was able to offer the best possible price in the liquidation of guilders and the acquisition of francs – '

'Which is true. Declan has explained to you the score with the guilders, which is just fine – '

'And the francs?'

Ansen turned to Declan, who spoke up: 'I'd like a few moments with Mr Ansen to make a call or two?'

They stood into the adjacent office, white-faced, and closed the door. 'What the hell is going on here?' Ansen hissed. 'You *do* have the francs?' A shadow of desperate doubt hung in his expression.

Declan dialled Shane and at last Jimmy Destry was on the line. Declan spoke in a clipped, steeled tone. 'Jimmy, do you recall I told you I wanted to work your position in that off-the-run stuff, the francs?' Leonard Ansen took up the next-door phone and listened in.

'No, I don't recall,' Jimmy came back.

'I told you, Jimmy. More than once – '

'I don't know what you're doing! You pass by and say you can move the francs, then you don't mention it again. What do you think I'm going to do? So I move them myself. A nice mid-market position, to First Manhattan. I made some money.'

'Stephanie Keys,' Ansen whispered dully. 'She must have tapped into our position and jumped it.'

'Jimmy, you bastard . . .'

But recriminations were useless; Stephanie Keys had the francs at a knockdown and was offering a package to blow out Shane Longman. It was *fait accompli*.

They rang off and Declan paced like a caged cat, cursing Jimmy. Ansen sat, breathless. 'What's the matter with you, Declan?' he said, voice full of pain. 'Your eyes are open. You see the blunders of judgement Sirkka and the others make. You know what a fine-line business this is. You know a miscalculation of a dollar or a split-second costs dearly. And you mess *this one* up. You and Jimmy are equally to blame. There's no excuse. You didn't communicate and communication is everything within a team.' He shook his head, lost with emotion. 'I spend half a year fantasizing about an account like PPF and when I get it I give it lock and stock to you. And you assist our biggest competitor to take it away from us . . .'

Recriminations were useless. They sat in silence for

a full five minutes, then Ansen stood up and sighed and moved back to face Trelaunay and Mason. Declan tagged along, wordless.

'I know you are men who like to call a spade a spade,' Ansen began, dry-mouthed. 'So all I can say is, we appear to have miscalculated aspects of the market. Despite what Declan predicted about the value of francs – and I do think he was reasonably realistic – I would like to recommend a reconsideration on the basis of Gilts – '

'We are not interested in reconsidering, Mr Ansen.' Mason had the face of a fighter. 'And we would like to remind you that you are contractually bound to execute the deal as outlined in our mandate. So the choice is yours. Do you wish to see through a guilders-francs arrangement? – and that of course assumes you will match this better offer. Or do you wish to withdraw?'

Ted Trelaunay stepped aggressively into the fray: 'Just a minute, Denzil. I do not propose to let Shane Longman off the hook so easily. To my thinking, they have no choice.' He reached for the intercom switch. 'Unless our lawyers see it otherwise?'

Ansen sucked in his gut and spoke with great dignity: 'There's no need for lawyers. I accept that we have an ethical as well as a contractual commitment to fulfil. First Manhatten are only able to make their offer because they picked up a large chunk of French government paper at a very favourable – and fluke – midmarket price. In order to execute our commitment to you we at Shane shall have to finance a repurchase which the bank will underwrite fully.'

Trelaunay jerked upright in response, surprised at the speed of Ansen's decision. The difference would cost Shane Longman half a million dollars, big bucks, even for the purchase of restored reputation.

Mason's truculence melted away. 'What went wrong, Leonard? This laddie sounded competent.'

Ansen looked at Declan, who couldn't meet his eye, then back at the Welshman. 'It's a crooked world. My man here played it straight, too straight, too trusting. I'll have to teach him to be ready for the wolves.'

Mason had been around enough to know a little of Stephanie Keys and her methods. He gave a twisted smile. 'You stand by Mr McConnochie?'

'Like I stand by this deal. Loyalty and commitment make the world go around. Mistakes are just mistakes.'

'Even if they cost half a million?'

'What's money? Just paper.'

Down the street Ansen was too edgy to go back to the car. He began to walk – aimless – and Declan fell in step. They covered two, three miles, shouldering blindly through the early crowds, lost in their own connected worlds.

At a magazine-and-hamburgers stall Ansen stopped and called for two coffees. They sat on tall wooden stools, incongruous alongside the denim scruffs chomping their breakfast burgers.

'It's hard to find the words,' Declan began. 'I wanted very much not to let you down on this one – '

'It wasn't all your fault. Nor Jimmy's. Stephanie Keys played dirty. She tapped into our information and found out what she wanted. Then she homed in on Destry, our weakest link – '

Declan thought of the computer tangles, and all the dark rumours running amok. 'You don't mean she broke the access code . . . ? I mean, she couldn't be so insane . . . ?'

Ansen shrugged. 'Somehow she found out.'

'Why didn't you tell Trelaunay and Mason? Spill it all out?'

'They're big boys, Declan. And this is a nasty world.' He smiled for the first time in what seemed like a century. 'And no, I will not accept your resignation. I invested in you. Wendy invested in you. Both of us want to see our investment grow.'

'What about the half million? When Lee Wolf gets to hear about it – '

'Let me worry about Lee Wolf.' He winked. 'Anyway, what he doesn't know won't hurt him. What he will hear will be the Stephanie Keys angle, and the hint of espionage, pure and simple. Who knows, unfolding events with the computers might colour that picture persuasively? Ms Keys might have a very serious case to answer.'

They finished their coffees. Felix had tailed them in the Rolls and now he pulled up near the hamburger stall and gently trumped the horn to signal his presence. Ansen threw a pound tip to the kid tending the stall and steered Declan into the Rolls. A knot of long-haired denims raised their bleary heads, pined for the revolution, and went about their burgers.

Felix steered towards the City.

Epilogue

Dover opened its arms to Gabriel Romero Mara and the Shane Longman invasion plan in the last chill days of autumn. The townsfolk turned out in numbers, unseasonal sightseers poured in from Folkestone, from Ramsgate, from the ferries. Local tradefolk dashed to offer their services cheaply, or for free. And the media swooped to chart it all.

Leonard Ansen stood on the soft green turf at a vantage point overlooking the dramatic construction and closed his ears to the roar of Jet Ranger props and the heckling humour of the children gathered. Below him the gallant white cliffs hid their feet in the rich creamy sea, a sugar icing vision that had been, two thousand years ago, Caesar's first sight of England. He looked north, past the virgin pebble beaches of Walmer and Deal, beaches the Riviera would pay the earth for, towards the North Foreland and the mist-shrouded wall of Ramsgate. To the south the coast stretched forever, a perfect checkerboard of white and green, fringed by the spectacular twelve-fathom channel of the Inner Leads and, further out, the liners, merchantmen, schuyts and fish boats of twenty nations. The sky domed blue, gulls wheeled – who knows, maybe bluebirds even? – and the sun shone to order.

'Make you proud to be English?' a voice echoed his thoughts. It was James Farrell, huddled in an overcoat against the inshore breeze, looking a little tireder, as he seemed to do every day now. They had come down in a fleet of cars – six executives including Farrell, Wolf and Ansen, plus Wendy, Max and a handful of dealers off the floor – to celebrate the inaugural moves in an historic artistic construction. Everyone had surrendered to the jollity of the occasion from the outset, making a day of it; everyone, that was, except Ansen. Farrell had asked him to share the executive Rolls, but Ansen had politely declined; he wanted to be alone, to ride this last wave unassisted, to be there, alone with his thoughts, when the first baby steps of a bold new Shane Longman were taken.

Wolf, of course, was sullen. Only yesterday they had slugged out the issue of the PPF half million and Wolf had fought with knuckles and feet to bring Ansen down.

Though the computer systems were functioning with their usual steady precision, the investigation into the possibility of an access code break-in was still running, with a specialist team headed up by Hannah and a Reuters expert unravelling every separate information chain for the last three months and comparing outside market movements. How nasty was Stephanie Keys, and to what depths had she stooped? These questions remained unanswered and vital; the mysteries – and the guesswork – were enough to cover Leonard Ansen's hide. For now.

As yesterday's meeting broke up Wolf cornered Ansen in the hall and swore, 'You're upending everything that Shane has stood for. You won't get away with it. I intend to pull this bank back in line, one way or the other.'

'So you'll skip the Mara sponsorship opening?'

But of course Wolf did not skip the opening. He was there blazing confidence, embracing the chance to dally with the media boys, posing for endless photographs, posing with Mara even.

'You've got to hand it to him,' Farrell said as they watched Wolf return to his car, handshaking to right and left. 'He won't lie down.'

'That makes two of us.'

Farrell spoke again but the roar of a low-flying helicopter – one of the two transporting the scaffold structure up the cliff face – drowned him. He semaphored smilingly and bade Ansen adieu.

Gabriel Romero Mara was standing with Max, Wendy and a group of reporters on the video observation platform, the radio control centre for the helicopters and the workers. From here the climbers, riggers and artists by proxy would receive the short wave instructions that would call on them to risk their lives in the interests of art – and a bank's publicity. Wendy spotted Ansen, waved to him, and ran down the steps.

'Bored already?' she said. 'The artist hasn't even touched his canvas!'

'Just thinking.' He sauntered along the cliff, away from the choppers. 'What dreams Caesar must have had when he walked these meadows. It must be the air: makes me think that anything is possible.'

'Isn't it?'

'I don't know.' He stopped and looked into her eyes. 'How's your apartment move? I haven't had time to pay you the courtesy of asking.'

'It's fine. Exhausting. But that's what I expected. Changes are always a struggle.'

'You need a rest.'

'I know. Me, Sirkka, Hudson, you – '

He gave her that devilish smile, the smile that put excitement – and alarm bells – into her blood. 'Did I tell you I won a holiday? In a golf tournament. A weekend trip to Paris. The George V, all expenses – '

'Sounds splendid.'

'For two.'

'Even better.'

'I was thinking . . .' His eyes roamed to the garrulous group of Shane traders fifty yards away and beyond, to where a solitary couple were wrapped in murmured conversation. 'I gave Declan no birthday present.'

She bent her head and captured his eye and held it. She gave back the devilish smile. 'I think you're right,' she said. 'Declan needs cheering up.'

At that moment Max called out, inviting Wendy to join him on one of the Jet Rangers gearing up to drop a dummy swathe of silk. Ansen watched her stride away, admiring her wit and her wisdom – *and* her classic legs – and then he walked to the cliff edge where Declan sat with Michelle.